THE

Gam

DOUGLAS HARDING

This book was digitised with the help of the following wonderful volunteers:
Al Matanovic, Bill Gillies, Dave Croce, Jim Van Meggelen, Mary Blight, Nelly Beraud Edmeads, Richard Lang, Stephanie Klauser.

Published by The Shollond Trust
87B Cazenove Road
London N16 6BB
England

headexchange@gn.apc.org
www.headless.org

The Shollond Trust is a UK charity, no 1059551

Copyright © The Shollond Trust 2016

Design and conversion to book by rangsgraphics.com

ISBN 978-1-908774-22-4

DEDICATION

This book is dedicated to the memory of Alan Rowlands (1929—2012) in gratitude for his generous support of The Shollond Trust.

CONTENTS

PREFACE	i
INTRODUCTION	1
HOW WE PLAY—GUIDANCE FOR THE LEADER	3
PROLOGUE	7
WHY WE PLAY THESE GAMES	7
GEAR	15
WARNING	17
PART 1 BASIC GAMES	19
1 THE HIDDEN KINGDOM	21
2 WHERE TO FIND THE KINGDOM	25
3a HOW TO LOSE SHAPE	29
3b HOW TO TAKE SHAPE	33
4 HOW TO OPEN YOUR SINGLE EYE	37
5 YOUR BIRTHDAY PRESENT	41
6 YOUR NEIGHBOUR AS YOURSELF	49
7 THE MAGIC PEARL	53
8 AN OUT-OF-THE-BODY EXPERIENCE	55
9 THE MAGIC MIRROR	59
10 OVER THE WORLD'S EDGE	63
11 CLEANED OUT	67
12 THE HEAD OF THE CHURCH	71
EVALUATION	75
PART 2 DEVELOPED GAMES	77
13 SORT YOURSELF OUT	79

14 HOW TO LIGHT UP THE WORLD	83
15 TREASURE HUNT	87
16 THE EMPEROR, THE DRUNKARD, THE TEAPOT, AND THE GHOST	91
17 YOUR SIDE OF EVERY STORY	101
18 CONFIDENCE TRICKS	105
19a HOW TO SEE GOD	111
19b HOW TO HEAR GOD	115
20 THE PRINCE, THE SERPENT, THE PEARL	121
21 HOW TO SPIN THE WORLD	131
22 FREEHAND, FOOTLOOSE	135
23 HOW TO LET YOURSELF GO	139
24 TO THE FAR COUNTRY	143
25 DEAR GOD	151
26 AS IT WAS IN THE BEGINNING	155
27 WHAT IS YOUR REAL NAME?	163
28 ALL CREATURES GREAT—AND SMALL?	167
29a THE SECRET DOOR	177
29b INTO THE ENCHANTED GARDEN	181
30 HOW TO HEAL	191
31 HOW TO CAST OUT DEVILS	197
32 SUN OF MY SOUL	201
33 THE FOUNTAINHEAD	207
34 THE VINE	215
35 THE LIVING BREAD	219
36 THE CROSS	223

PART 3 ADDITIONAL GAMES	227
37 ORANGES AND LEMONS	229
38 CURE FOR SHYNESS?	231
39 MULBERRY BUSH	233
40 NURSERY CHAIRS	235
41 CUMBYA	237
42 THE WISE MEN OF GOTHAM	239
43 FIELD SPORTS	241
44 HOW GOOD IS YOUR CHINESE?	245
45 FULL NAME AND ADDRESS	247
46 THE KEY OF THE KINGDOM	249
EPILOGUE	251
SCHOOLS FOR THE KINGDOM	253
REFERENCES	259

PREFACE

The Hidden Gospel presents an exciting new interpretation of the teachings of Jesus. In this workshop manual Douglas Harding invites you to do his breakthrough experiments and experience, directly, the Reality that Jesus was talking about.

Harding had a deep feeling for Jesus. Born in 1909, Harding was brought up in a fundamentalist Christian sect, the Exclusive Plymouth Brethren, whose members put Jesus at the centre of their lives. Though he left the Brethren when he was 21, rejecting their narrow dogmatism and intolerance, Harding knew the Gospels like the back of his hand, and retained a profound love and respect for Jesus. He admired him for so courageously living and speaking the truth, even in the face of death: the truth that we are both human and divine.

In the early 1940s, after years of enquiry, Harding suddenly saw who he really was in a modern scientific way—he saw that, though he appeared human at six feet, at zero distance he was nothing at all. Nothing full of everything. Then in the late '60s Harding invented his experiments—awareness exercises which physically point at what we are at zero distance, the boundless, timeless Reality behind all our appearances. They make the experience of our central Reality—the Ground of Being—

available to anyone willing to look. They are a scientific response to the spiritual question, 'Who am I?'

It was natural that at some point Harding would combine the ancient teachings of Jesus, so influential in his life and in Western civilization, with his experiments—with modern science—for science had led him to the Reality that Jesus lived and died for. In *The Hidden Gospel* Harding showed how the teachings of Jesus made sense in scientific terms—including some teachings that sound plainly untrue, or at best metaphorical. When Jesus spoke about having a 'single eye' and of his body being 'full of light', what did he mean? Anyone looking at him would have seen he had two eyes and his body was not made of light. But carry out Harding's 'single eye' experiment and within a few moments all is clarified, not through debate but by seeing—seeing that your eye is single, that your body is made of light. Now the words of Jesus make sense.

Although *The Hidden Gospel* introduces a modern interpretation of Jesus, giving him a new voice in today's world, hopefully it will reach people beyond the Christian world—and therefore play a part in resolving some of the religious conflict in our world. As well as demonstrating where the findings of science and the goal of Christianity meet—in our central Reality, in the indivisible Ground of Being—in principle it demonstrates where science and all religions meet. The experiments make it possible for anyone to see and consciously be in the Centre, in the place from which we can view our religious differences—or any other differences—but not be caught up in them. Given the conflict flowing from the clashes between religions, a growing awareness of the unity that exists beneath our differences is an urgent priority.

The Hidden Gospel, completed in 1974 but published now for the first time in paperback, is for anyone, from whatever tradition, who wishes to find out what Jesus really meant, not by debating his teachings but by experiencing for themselves the boundless core of their own being, and then seeing how clearly and beautifully Jesus described this experience, this Reality. This book does not appeal to Jesus as a religious authority who tells you what to believe but as a fellow traveller who found 'the pearl of great price' and, with great courage, did his best to share it with others.

Richard Lang

INTRODUCTION

The present manual is certainly unique. Nothing like it has ever been attempted in the Christian field. It takes seriously Jesus' insistence that, until we grown-ups turn round and become like little children, we have no chance of entering the Kingdom. All children play games. Here, then, is a wide choice of games by which—having failed, perhaps, to think or feel our way into the Kingdom—we may at last play our way in. Each game takes one or more of the sayings of Jesus and tests them in a workshop (or playroom) setting, relying on simple, childlike perception and action instead of the talk so characteristic of adults.

As for children—of, say, 10 or over, in and out of school and Sunday-school—this is their secret world.

No wonder every child loves a secret: he has the essential secret. The immense Kingdom that the childlike discover within is invisible to outsiders, and its Gospel is necessarily a hidden or 'apochryphal' one. This manual claims to give direct access to that clear insight which underlies the gospel texts—including those which orthodoxy has done its best to suppress. It offers nothing less than initiation into what must have been the central experience of Jesus—if we assume that he practised what he preached, and was himself like a little child.

The games or initiation-exercises are suitable for any number of players between 5 and 30 or more. Most of them can, however, be managed effectively on your own. In any case they aren't for doing just once or twice. Whether you experience them as guided meditation or worship or therapy or experimental science (the science of the 1st person) or a special sort of fun and games—or a mixture of all of these—they are likely to grow on you.

Douglas Harding.

HOW WE PLAY—GUIDANCE FOR THE LEADER

The ideal number of players is anything between 8 and 20; however, 6 is not too few and 30 not too many. And if at present you lack any friends at all who are able to join you, go ahead nevertheless. Most of the games can be managed on your own, and where a partner is essential your mirror will supply him. Where a game definitely cannot be played solitaire-fashion, the minimum number of players (excluding the Leader) is indicated.

Dress comfortably. Slacks are preferred to skirts, open-necked shirts to buttoned-up ones. Shoes off.

A quiet, uncluttered, carpeted room with floor-cushions and a few chairs is recommended. All but the infirm should sit on the floor: getting down to the child's physical level makes it easier to get to his mental level. It's as if our grown-up intellectual smog starts around 4 feet from the floor, and below that lies the clearer air we used to breathe.

A games' Leader is required. His jobs are to marshal the players into the correct formation or set-up for the game, then to read out its title and text(s), to conduct the players through the game, and at the end to re-read the text(s). He should speak very distinctly and slowly, with ample pauses. Directions meant only for him are printed in italics, to distinguish them from what he is to read out to the others. Passages which are not essential, and which some adults—and even some children—are likely to find rather difficult, are printed in smaller type, to indicate that they may be omitted without blunting the point of the game.

The Leader will find that all but the simplest games—until he knows them well enough to improvise—require him to direct proceedings from outside, without fully joining in.

Another function of the Leader is to see the rules aren't entirely forgotten, and to bring players back to the point. The only hope of settling a real difficulty, or a disagreement arising out of a game, is to re-play the game more attentively, or go on hopefully to the next one. Argument is futile, for the raison d'être of the game is to get behind the smoke-screen of talk, to direct, non-verbal experience.

How should the Leader plan his programme?

In principle, each game is self-sufficient and can give entry to the kingdom within. But in practice the games support and supplement one another; their impact together is much greater than piecemeal; and their variety meets the needs of players of different temperaments. Normally, therefore, a play-session will consist of all—or most—of the basic 12 games of Part I, lasting some 2 to 3 hours, plus a selection from Parts II and III, depending on the time available and the age and inclinations of the players.

If the games are familiar to some of the players, so much

the better. Children's games don't suffer by repetition; and neither do ours, provided they are making their point—a point inaccessible to memory. Each is then played as if for the first time, and becomes an ever-renewed discovery (or meditation, or celebration, or act of worship, or therapeutic exercise) which actually gains by repetition.

Of course, to the degree that the Leader is familiar with the repertoire, he will leave his selection largely or wholly to the inspiration of the moment.

It is suggested that the rest periods should be brief, frequent, and silent.

To break up a long session (one lasting a day or more) the Leader may decide to allocate an hour or two to an Interlude—a 'relaxed' and informal period for musical, athletic, or other events, preferably held out-of-doors. Part III (Additional Games) offers some suggestions.

Particularly when a long session is planned, involving players new to the games, no-one should be pressed to stay through to the end. Any who are finding the games meaningless or threatening should be encouraged to leave, and if possible alternative programmes—of quite a different sort—should be provided for them. It is often better that 'Games for the Kingdom' should form part of a conference (summer school, week-end convention) rather than the whole of it, so that the members' options are open and nothing is forced on them. This precaution is important because, as the Leader will soon find, our games go deep, and for some are as disturbing as for others they are illuminating and healing. Not all are ready for this medicine. To thrust it down the throats of unwilling subjects is a kind of violence, and no wonder if the reactions are violent. Though the kingdom itself is one and the same for all comers, the ways in are many and diverse. There is a right moment and a right gate for every man, and trying to push him headlong through one's favourite entry is not only insulting, but futile.

PROLOGUE

WHY WE PLAY THESE GAMES

Jesus said: "Unless you turn round and become like children, you will never enter the kingdom of Heaven."

Children have fun. They play games. These games are, however, not in the least flippant or trivial: the child takes them very seriously. They are his style, his natural disposition. They are his way of learning-by-doing, and indispensable for his healthy development.

Here, accordingly, we take Jesus at his word and present some games which, to the degree that we drop our grown-up defences, may indeed give entry to the kingdom. They could hardly be more serious—or more light-hearted. (Light-hearted is here no metaphor, but just what they are—as we shall see.)

They are for anyone to play—anyone, that is, who is over (say) 10, but isn't yet so adult that he has altogether lost touch with the child in him. In particular, they are intended for 3 kinds of people: first, those committed Christians who are prepared to find new meaning in their Master's words, even if it comes to them from outside the Church; second, those would-be Christians who regretfully find much of his teaching obscure or unacceptable as it is commonly presented; and third, those non-Christians who would like to get to know him at depth, by getting to know themselves at depth.

Each game is linked—more or less loosely—with the reported words of Jesus. Its precise relevance to those words, as quoted here from the Gospels[1], can be judged only by actually playing that game. Nobody is likely to find all the games helpful or to the point. But if only one or two bring some endlessly repeated text to new life, why then the rest may cheerfully be put aside for the present; or perhaps appreciated for their secular message, outside a Christian context.

As a matter of fact, all our games come to the same thing, or rather No-thing. All are designed to celebrate (in their very different ways, to suit different temperaments) one and the same central Simplicity. There are many gates to the kingdom, but nobody needs more than one to come in by. Any of our games, provided its point is directly seen—and not merely grasped at by the mind—is enough. The others are then confirmatory rather than necessary.

Of course we are (following the example of the great Christian mystics) testing the scriptures by our experience rather than our experience by the scriptures, and freely

---

[1] From the Gospel of Thomas, and occasionally from other sources, as well as from the four canonical Gospels. Textual references are given at the end of the book. In rendering the texts into modern English, use has been made of the New English Bible, and other translations.

adapting them to our own purposes. Is this justified? Let's play these games with an open mind and heart, try them out in everyday life, and come to our own conclusions. Do they lead to greater love, to the truth which sets us free? Of course we are bound to ask about each game: 'Did Jesus mean anything like this, at the time he spoke those words?' No-one can be sure. In some instances, the chances are that he did not. But there is a question we can answer with confidence: 'Do we find the message of this game to be true now, and important, and beautiful?' If so, it belongs to his kingdom, no matter how far it deviates from the traditional interpretation of the text which we have linked with that game.

This book may be regarded as a detective story come to life: a mystery, and its solution—by no means an arm-chair solution. It puts forward and actually tests—using a wide variety of experiments—a simple hypothesis about Jesus Christ. The hypothesis is as follows:-

Practising what he preached, Jesus himself became as a little child, and remained so throughout his adult life. This meant that he found in himself two natures: the human grown-up and the divine child; the outside story and the inside; the 3rd person and the 1st; the flesh others saw him to be at (say) 50 inches and the spirit he saw himself to be at 0 inches; Jesus, the local carpenter and odd-job man, and the cosmic Christ, the I AM, the indwelling Godhead, the Light that lights every man.

Sometimes he spoke in terms of his particular manhood, sometimes in terms of his universal Godhood. But his inspiration was the Godhood, and his mission was to share it with his followers. What was so true for him had to be true for all.

They did not find it so. Too complicated and adult to look within and see what he meant, his followers inevitably misunderstood the core of his teaching, and their account of it could only be a garbled one. In particular, failing to distinguish clearly between the outer appearance and the inner Reality, they claimed for their Master an exclusive divinity which he never claimed. They raised Jesus on a pedestal that belongs only to Christ. They separated his I AM from all others—as if there could be others.

No wonder, then, that the Gospel story turned out to be a maze of puzzles and contradictions. The remarkable thing is, in fact, that so much of his basic inspiration can be recognised (often in curiously oblique forms, in metaphors that aren't metaphors at all but precise statements of fact, in attempted rationalisations and dilutions) and can be pieced together into a convincing whole once we have the key. This indispensable key is the one he presses on us again and again: "Unless you turn round and become like children, you will never enter the kingdom." And (we may add) you will never spot the many clues, scattered throughout the Gospels, to what it means to be childlike. To the thoroughly adult mind, Jesus Christ must remain a stranger.

Jesus didn't give up hope of being understood. He spoke of an on-going revelation, of a time when the Spirit will guide us into all truth. Is that time over? Is that revelation running out? Doesn't every generation need to re-discover, in its own unique terms, the Everlasting Gospel? In any case, it has no alternative. Confronted by so many contradictory elements in Christian literature and tradition, the Spirit in us has to be its own authority, to sift and discriminate all things by its own Light. It is bound by no formula or institution; it is free to try things out, to make brand new discoveries, to start all over again, to shock deeply. The letter kills, the Spirit gives life: and life is unpredictable, often heretical, sometimes outrageous. It leaves room for the unknown to happen in.

The Spirit is the Spirit of truth. When Jesus' pronouncements seem irrational, and flagrantly to contradict the facts, 3 alternatives are open to us. (1) We may, relying on reason, reject as impossible such difficult dogmas as—for instance—the miracle of the eucharist (the bread and the wine being changed into his true body and blood); or (2) we may, against all reason, "believe because it is impossible"; or (3) we may, avoiding these grown-up extremes, ask in what simple sense the dogma can be true, and just how the miracle of transubstantiation can actually be observed—by those who turn round and become as honest as little children. (Game 35, in fact, asks precisely this question—and, as we may find, answers it beyond any doubt. It shows how more honest scepticism, more intellectual integrity—not less—can enable the sincere rationalist to sup happily with the Lord.)

One more instance out of many: somewhat rashly, it would seem, Jesus promises his followers that they will move mountains. To a child, a mountain is a solid object on the horizon, not a metaphorical obstacle. Again we shall investigate (in Game 29b) in what simple sense his promise is immediately and generously granted—to the truly childlike.

As we work though our programme we may again and again discover that, directly we bring to the Gospels this childlike attitude, we get at once to their heart, and that what we find there turns out to be perfectly sensible and manifestly true—but only to the innocent eye. Our games set out to show how accessible the deepest things really are, if only we can be simple and brave enough to doubt what we think and trust what we see. For what is true spirituality, after all, but humility before the facts as clearly presented by God at this moment to the unsophisticated, rather than a proud (and servile) insistence upon the ideas of men as elaborated over the centuries? The only real heresy is complicating the uncomplicated, wilfully turning a blind eye to the obvious, the self-evident, the given-by-God-now, the immediate, the child's view—in the interests of some system that is just the opposite of all these things.

What we call our Games for the Kingdom, then, are nothing more or less than exercises in attention. Attention, without prejudice, to 'how it is'. Attention to what's given now, on present evidence, dropping (as far as possible) memory and anticipation, imagination, hear-say, and every sort of pious and impious opinion. Attention, above all, to what's given here, when one dares at last to turn round and explore that immense and all-but-unknown realm—the kingdom within, the very spot one stands on. Is this indeed holy ground, in fact the only holy ground? Can one truthfully say, echoing the Patriarch, "The Lord is in this place, and I didn't know it. This is none other than the house of God, and this is the gate of Heaven"? Our exercises in attention should enable us to answer such questions beyond any doubt.

GEAR

This list of apparatus assumes 12 players. It omits the whole of the games in Part III, and those parts of games in Parts I and II which are marked 'Optional'.

GENERAL

Writing materials.
Drawing materials, including cards.
Scissors and string.
At least 4 chairs.

PART 1

Game	Quantity	Description
6	6	Paper bags, approx. 12in x 12in, bottoms cut off.
9	12	Hand-mirrors
11	12	Cards, approx. 12in x 12in, with head-shaped, head-sized holes.

PART 2

Game	Quantity	Description
13	12+	Self-adhesive spots, 5 colours.
16	1	Teapot or similar vessel.
	2	Masks (one lunatic, the other ghastly) in boxes.
	1	Paper bag as in Game 6.
18	6	Paper cut-outs, say 9in x 6in.
19b	1	Gong, bell, or musical instrument.
25	1	Candle on incombustible tray or very large dish.
26	1	Portable clock, preferably with second hand
	1	Current calendar
28		Any creatures available and willing (or obliged) to stay awhile.
	1	Punnet of garden cress.
	12	Buttered biscuits or pieces of bread.
	1	Mirror
29b	12	Pieces of transparent blue acetate or glass, say 3in x 1in.
	12	Pieces of transparent red acetate or glass, say 3in x 1in.
	2	White cups or beakers.
31	12	Paper bags as in Game 6.
35	12	Any morsels to eat.

WARNING

READING ABOUT THESE GAMES INSTEAD OF PLAYING THEM IS LIKE EATING THE MENU INSTEAD OF THE DINNER

Most of them can be played on your own and where a partner is needed your mirror can supply him.

PART 1 BASIC GAMES

A play-session will normally comprise most, if not all, the 12 games of Part I (lasting, with brief rests, 2 hours or so), plus a selection of more elaborate games from Parts 2 and 3—as time allows and the interests of the players indicate.

1 THE HIDDEN KINGDOM

Jesus said:

Thank you, Father, lord of Heaven and earth, for hiding these things from the wise and the prudent, and revealing them to babes.

The kingdom of God belongs to such as these. I tell you, whoever does not accept the kingdom of God like a little child will never enter it.

When he, the Spirit of truth has come, he will guide you into all truth.

The Spirit of truth will be with you for ever. The world cannot receive him, because the world neither sees him nor knows him; but you know him, because he dwells with you and is in you.

The truth will set you free.

***

Time: 10 mins.
Gear: None.
Set-up: Sit in a circle on the floor.

* *Read out the texts above. Then read out the following very slowly, with ample pauses:*

1 THE GAMES

Jesus says that the kingdom is a secret one, hidden from the grown-up world. He says that, until we turn round and become like little children, we have no chance of entering the kingdom.

All children play games. The games are fun, and very serious.

So we are going to play games.

Supposing we have failed, so far, to gain admission as adults, let's see if we can play our way into the hidden kingdom.

2 THE RULES

All games have rules. We have 5. Let's do our best:

(1) To avoid vague and difficult words which only adults understand.

(2) To concern ourselves with what's present in this room, and not with the world of absent people and places and times.

(3) To rely on ourselves, on what we can see and hear and taste and handle, rather than what we think or imagine or remember or have been told.

(4) To settle our differences by further experimenting, by doing rather than arguing.

(5) To play these games with an open and childlike mind, prepared to be made a fool of by the facts, and to bow to the truth—even when it clashes with our religious opinions and the world's common sense.

3 THE PLAYERS

Having agreed these 5 rules, let's introduce ourselves.

Let's go round the circle, clockwise, saying our names in the form "I am Mary", "I am John", or whatever, but don't leave out the I AM, which is our Common Denominator.

The naming completed, proceed:

Now we know one another's names. Or have we forgotten some already?

Never mind! No-one has forgotten the I AM—the name we all share.

Repeat the texts:

Jesus said:

Thank you, Father, lord of Heaven and earth, for hiding these things from the wise and the prudent, and revealing them to babes.

The kingdom of God belongs to such as these. I tell you, whoever does not accept the kingdom of God like a little child will never enter it.

When he, the Spirit of truth has come, he will guide you into all truth.

The Spirit of truth will be with you for ever. The world cannot receive him, because the world neither sees him nor knows him; but you know him, because he dwells with you and is in you.

The truth will set you free.

***

* *Instructions to the Leader are printed in italics, to distinguish them from what he reads out to the players. In subsequent games, this particular instruction at the beginning of each chapter (to read out the texts, etc.,) is not repeated.*

2 WHERE TO FIND THE KINGDOM

Jesus said:

Unless you turn round…. You will never enter the kingdom of Heaven.

If they say to you, 'Look, the kingdom is in the sky, then the birds will get there before you. If they say to you, 'It is in the sea', then the fish will get there before you. In fact, the kingdom is within you.

The kingdom of God does not come with outward show. Nor shall they say, 'Look, here it is', or 'There it is'; for, in fact, the kingdom of God is within you.

***

Time: 10 mins.
Gear: None.
Set-up: As before.

Something immensely valuable has been hidden in this room. I want you to find it.

In fact, it isn't a thing at all, but a sort of clearing, a secret empty place, rather like those strange Black Holes which astronomers have recently discovered in the sky.

Only this Hole certainly isn't black, and it's immense.
If it's a kingdom, it's one without frontiers and without a pollution problem.
It has been called 'the country of everlasting clearness'.

Get up and start looking.

Move around the room, pointing at *things* one after another, noticing how each has a certain shape,
and colour,
and texture,
and size.
Go on searching, till your finger points at what has no shape or colour or texture or size,

At no-thing,

At this mysterious region, this clear country.

And when you have found it, don't give the game away, but stop pointing and sit down again in the circle—this time facing outwards.

Game 2 Where to Find the Kingdom

After a minute or two, any who are still looking around are asked to join the others on the floor, in a neat circle, facing outwards.

All point *upwards*, noticing what you are pointing at.

Now all point *outwards*, noticing what you are pointing at.

Now all point *downwards*, noticing what you are pointing at.

Now all point *inwards*, to the centre of the circle, to your own 'face', noticing what you are pointing at.

Drop memory, and just attend to what's given now.

Keep on pointing.

To find your way to an earthly kingdom—like Belgium or Holland or Denmark—you need to know its compass bearings.

It's exactly the same if you want to find your way to the kingdom of Heaven.

Suppose you are now facing North: in what direction, precisely, does the kingdom of Heaven lie?

Keep on pointing, while I repeat our texts:

Jesus said:

Unless you turn round…. You will never enter the kingdom of Heaven.

If they say to you, 'Look, the kingdom is in the sky, then the birds will get there before you. If they say to you, 'It is in the sea', then the fish will get there before you. In fact, the kingdom is within you.

The kingdom of God does not come with outward show. Nor shall they say, 'Look, here it is', or 'There it is'; for, in fact, the kingdom of God is within you.

**

3a HOW TO LOSE SHAPE

Jesus said:

If your whole body is full of light, having no part dark, the whole shall be full of light, as when the bright shining of a candle gives you light.

When you make the two one,
and make the inside like the outside,
and the outside like the inside,
and the upper side like the under side,
and you make the man with the woman a single one,
so that the man is not a man and the woman is not a woman…
then you will go into the kingdom.

**

Time: 10 mins.
Gear: None.
Set-up: Tell the players to stand up and keep their eyes closed. Line them up, half facing one wall, the other half facing the opposite wall, so that each stands back-to-back with his partner and about 2 feet away from him. They then open their eyes.

Looking straight ahead and standing still and at ease, drop memory and imagination, and answer the following questions—but not out loud:

On present evidence, how many toes have you?

How many legs?

How many fingers?

How many arms?

Perhaps you can find some feelings there, but do they add up to feet and hands?

For all you can tell, couldn't they just as well belong to hooves or claws or wings or fins—or to anything at all?

How many heads do you have now—if any?

Again, what's happened to your 2 eyes?

Can you find any boundaries to yourself, any inside and outside, any place where you stop and the world begins?

What sex are you? Male or female or neither?

What age are you? Young or old or ageless?

On present evidence, are you any more a human being now than you are an atom, or a star, or a cloud, or a bird-of-paradise, or a gorilla?

Couldn't I, for all you know, be a magician who is now turning you into all these things, one after the other, and back again?

Will you ever know, for sure, what actually happened?

In fact, aren't you now utterly dissolved into the kingdom of light, with no speck of darkness or opacity remaining?

Repeat the texts:

Jesus said:

If your whole body is full of light, having no part dark, the whole shall be full of light, as when the bright shining of a candle gives you light.

When you make the two one,
and make the inside like the outside,
and the outside like the inside,
and the upper side like the under side,
and you make the man with the woman a single one,
so that the man is not a man and the woman is not a woman…
then you will go into the kingdom.

***

Instruct the players to remain exactly as they are, in readiness for the second half of the game.

3b HOW TO TAKE SHAPE

Jesus said:

Unless a grain of wheat falls into the ground and dies, it remains alone; but if it dies it brings forth a rich harvest.

He who finds his life shall lose it, and he that loses his life…. shall find it.

***

Time: 5 mins.
Gear: None.
Set-up: Continue standing in 2 rows, back-to-back.

Go on looking straight ahead.

You are now space, capacity, room.

Room for what?

Dead to all you imagined you were, you are alive—to what?

Turn round and face your partner.

Take him in.

Are you now the space for him to happen in?

Shapeless, to be shaped by him?

Dead, to be enlivened by him?

How could you help vanishing in his favour?

How could you find him, except by losing yourself?

How could he be present to you, if you weren't absent?

Aren't you now getting back in him what you lost in yourself?

Move round the room.

Take shape as the other players,
as a chair, a picture, a flower, the scene outside the window,
as anybody or anything you fancy.

Who, among the players, by thus dying to his solitary self,

is re-born as all the others?

Who, by surrendering so little, gets so much?

Do you *achieve* this self-naughting?

Aren't you just built that way?

Repeat the texts:

Jesus said:

Unless a grain of wheat falls into the ground and dies, it remains alone; but if it dies it brings forth a rich harvest.

He who finds his life shall lose it, and he that loses his life…. shall find it.

***

4 HOW TO OPEN YOUR SINGLE EYE

Jesus said:

If your eye is single, your whole body will be full of light.

Take the beam out of your own eye.

It is better to enter the kingdom of God with one eye than to keep two eyes and be thrown into hell.

***

Time: 7 mins.
Gear: None.
Set-up: Sit in a circle on the floor, facing inwards.

Point again to the kingdom within.

What is now looking out from the kingdom at that pointing finger?

Dropping memory and imagination, are there 2 eyes looking, or one 'eye', or (to be exact) no eyes at all?

If you are wearing glasses take them off and hold them at arm's length. (If you aren't, make up a spectacle-frame with your thumbs and forefingers.)

Notice how the two openings are divided by the piece that fits your nose.

Now put them on slowly, observing what happens to this nose-piece or 'beam'.

Outline with your arms the shape and extent of your single 'eye'—its edges are where your hands just disappear.

What's *your* side of this huge 'window'?

Can you find anybody looking through it?

Now try to imagine your 2-eyed face, as the others in the circle are now seeing it.

Really try to get that face together, right where you are.

Which do you prefer—actually seeing yourself as you now see yourself here (one-eyed and full of light and spotless), or trying to see yourself as they are seeing you (2-eyed and opaque and far from spotless)?

Which is more worrying, more like hell?

Repeat the texts:

Jesus said:

If your eye is single, your whole body will be full of light.

Take the beam out of your own eye.

It is better to enter the kingdom of God with one eye than to keep two eyes and be thrown into hell.

***

5 YOUR BIRTHDAY PRESENT AND HOW TO UNWRAP IT

Jesus said:

Nobody lights a lamp and then covers it with a basin.
There is nothing covered that shall not be revealed.

He who is near me is near the fire; and he who is far from me is far from the kingdom.

Lift the stone and there you will find me;
split the wood and there I am.

The disciples asked:
"When will you be visible to us and when shall we see you?"

Jesus replied:
"When you are stripped and are not ashamed."

***

Time: (Sections 1, 3, 5) 20 mins.
Gear: (Sections 1, 3, 5) A 'viewfinder'—i.e. a card with a pea-sized hole in it—or a camera (no film needed). A loaded Polaroid camera, with lenses for close-up shots, would be ideal.
Set-up: Seat the players at the sides, leaving the length of the room clear.
Note: If you are alone, go up to a wall-mirror with your viewfinder, instead of to A.

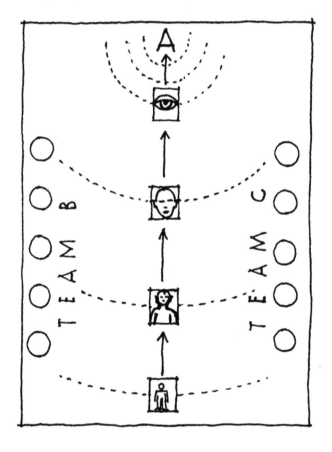

Do *you* see yourself as empty space?

Well, *we* see you as a solid lump.

Which is right?

Does our story make yours untrue? Can they be reconciled?

Let's see whether, in fact, there's any contradiction between what *we* make of you at (say) 6 feet, and what *you* make of you at 0 feet.

1 UNWRAPPING THE PRESENT

Your original birthday present, given to you when you were 0, is the best one you ever had. Why not, then, undo the parcel?

Would anyone like some help with the unwrapping?

A volunteers, and is told to stand at the far end of the room. You, the Leader, stand at the other end and get him in the viewfinder of your camera (or the hole in your card, held up to your eye), and address him:

What you *really* are, over there, I'm in no position to say.

But *here,* I make you out to be a whole human being, against some background. So I take this (imaginary/real) photograph of you, develop it instantly, and leave it here on the floor to mark the spot, say ... feet *(estimate distance)* from you, where you strike me as being a person called ..... *(give name)*.

Now I move forward, keeping you in my sights, and come to this place where you register as half human—or half a human—and I take another picture of you and leave it here to mark the spot.

Now I move forward again, and come to this place where you register as just a face, still with a name attached to it.

Repeating the exercise, I come to where you are one nameless eye.

And now I come to a place where you are revealed as a non-human, colourless, shapeless blur.

If we had the time and the optical equipment, and I moved still nearer to you, the blur would read as (say) an eyelash, then as a cell, then as (say) a chromosome, then as a molecule, and so on.

And at every stage of my inward journey I could take a photographic record of the view—of you—till there was no view at all, and I was confronted with more-or-less empty space.

Even so, I would still be observing you from a distance.

However close I get, I'm still an outsider, not right where you are.

Only you are in a position to complete the unwrapping and say what's present—what your original birthday present is—at *no* distance from you.

How is it where you are?

You are the inside story of yourself, your own birthday present laid bare.

Your coverings got more and more shadowy and transparent as we removed them.

Can we add: more and more like what they cover— Emptiness itself?

2 (optional) UNWRAPPING THE OTHERS PRESENT

Team B, armed with viewfinders, advance towards stationary team C, each 'unwrapping the present' of his opposite number and reporting findings. Team C repeats the exercise, team B remaining stationary.

3 UNWRAPPING EVERYTHING

All players: go right up to anything in the room and see if you don't lose it on the way.

Does this suggest that all things, in themselves, are empty?

There's only one thing in this room that you can get right to the core of, and check its no-thingness.

Which thing is that?

Can you take it as a true sample of the other things in the world?

4 (optional) OUTDOOR GAME

Repeat Section 1 in a large open space such as a beach, where some of the more distant layers of A's appearances can be explored.

Actual photographs can be taken and set up on sticks in the sand.

The layers can be mapped and recorded by scribing circles in the sand, using one peg fixed at A, connected with string to a second peg which moves.

If A plays an instrument or sings, and wears a carnation, his wrappings of sound and smell—and touch, of course—can be investigated and included.

How would A strike us, viewed from a rising helicopter?

From a space-ship?

Don't all A's cosmic wrappings, from electron to galaxy, stick together as one laminated packing material—each layer dependent on the rest, and by itself flimsy indeed?

But again, who but A can tell us what these worldwide appearances are appearances of?

5 CONCLUSION

Are the following statements true?

When you go right up to things you find that the inside story of man, animal, wood, stone, is the same.

Everything you approach is consumed, layer by layer, in your fire, the fire of the kingdom.

When you yourself aren't ashamed to be stripped bare, you uncover the absolute truth of things, their naked, imperishable core.

From the start, your immense and perfect birthday gift has never been hidden from you.

Ultimately we have all been given one and the same Birthday Present—God himself.

Repeat the texts:

Jesus said:

Nobody lights a lamp and then covers it with a basin.

There is nothing covered that shall not be revealed.

He who is near me is near the fire; and he who is far from me is far from the kingdom.

Lift the stone and there you will find me;

split the wood and there I am.

The disciples asked:

"When will you be visible to us and when shall we see you?"

Jesus replied:

"When you are stripped and are not ashamed."

***

6 YOUR NEIGHBOUR AS YOURSELF

Jesus said:

The Son of Man has nowhere to lay his head.

There is no greater love than this, that a man should lay down his life for his friends.

Love your neighbour as yourself.

***

Time: 7 mins.
Set-up: Sit down in pairs.
Note: If you are alone, use a mirror in the bag.
Gear: Paper bags, the more translucent the better, roughly 12 ins. x 12 ins. Cut their bottoms off to form tubes, one for each 2 players.

Fit your face into one end of the bag, while your neighbour fits his face into the other.

Answer the following questions (not out loud), going by what's given now in the bag, not by what you remember or imagine:

(1) How many faces are there in the bag?

(2) Are you face-to-face, or face-to-NO-face, with your neighbour?

(3) Is your end of the bag closed, or open?

(4) Where have you laid—or mislaid—your head?

Come out for a breather,

now go back.

(5) Aren't you now laying down your humanity, your life, your thinghood, your very matter, for your neighbour? Isn't this death *total*—not merely the death of your flesh into its chemical components, but also *their* death into their physical components and beyond, down into absolute No-thingness? No doubt the *feelings* and *acts* of love have infinite degrees; their Basis has none.

(6) And isn't this basic death ever-renewed—not once-for-all but continual, because you are built that way?

Out of the bag again, confront your neighbour with outstretched arms.

Is it hard, at this moment, to love him as *yourself*?

Now try to get face-to-face with him, confronting his *seen* face with your *imagined* face.

To the extent that you succeed, isn't this an unloving refusal to make way for him, a rejection, a warning to him to keep off, a sort of hate? And a lie, since your very nature is to be wide open for him?

Repeat the texts:

Jesus said:

The Son of Man has nowhere to lay his head.

There is no greater love than this, that a man should lay down his life for his friends.

Love your neighbour as yourself.

***

7 THE MAGIC PEARL

Jesus said:

Here is another picture of the kingdom of Heaven. A merchant looking out for fine pearls found one of very special value; so he went and sold everything that he had, and bought it.

***

Minimum no. of players: 4.
Time: 5 mins.
Gear: None.
Set-up: Kneel in a neat circle.

Carefully count the knees you can find.

Now the trunks.

Now the heads.

Is this like a giant's wedding ring—uniform metal all round?

Or more like an engagement ring, with a priceless pearl set in it?

If so, point to the pearl.

Or an eternity ring, with pearls all round?

Repeat the text:

Jesus said:

Here is another picture of the kingdom of Heaven. A merchant looking out for fine pearls found one of very special value; so he went and sold everything that he had, and bought it.

***

8 HOW TO HAVE AN OUT-OF-THE-BODY EXPERIENCE

Jesus said:

If the light that is in you is darkness, how great is that darkness!

Clean the inside of the cup.

You are like tombs covered with whitewash; they look well from outside, but inside they are full of dead men's bones and all kinds of filth.

Seek for yourselves a place within for rest, so that you do not become a corpse.

Disciples: On what day does the new world come?

Jesus: What you are waiting for has come, but you do not recognise it.

***

Time: 8 mins.
Gear: None.
Set-up: None.

Around this time, players should be encouraged to raise any difficulties or objections.

Here is one that is sure to crop up:

"I know there's a head here because I can *feel* it. My senses tell me I'm in the body. I live in this mortal tenement, this house of clay, till I die."

Examine that curious structure resting on your neighbour's shoulders.

Now try to build on your own shoulders—by stroking, pinching, pummelling—a similar house of clay,
opaque,
coloured,
all-present-at-once.

Now try to collect yourself and take up residence.

Have you moved in yet?

Are you no longer at large, but shut up in some kind of house or prison or tomb? Or corpse?

If so, what's it like in there—dark as midnight, sticky, small, congested, stuffy, full of bones and all sorts of mess?

In fact, aren't you still clear and huge—room for the world to happen in?

Game 8 Out of Body Experience

In so far as you have one at all, isn't this great world your body?

- An onion-like body whose extremities (such as stars) are seen, whose less remote members (such as planes and birds) are also heard, whose near members (such as your clothes) are also felt, whose very near members (such as food) are also smelled and tasted, and whose empty core is revealed to every sense—as absence of sensation?

If you are trapped in a body, isn't it in this body?

And isn't even this one, rather, trapped in you?

Turn to your neighbour, and tangle your hands with his into a ball.

On present evidence, which of those fingers are yours?

Are you *in* some, and not the others?

Examine your feet. Are you more in them than in the carpet?

See if you are inside your wrist, yet outside your wristwatch.

People talk about having an out-of-the-body experience.

Have you had any other sort?

They look for the day when they will be let out of the prison of the body.

Hasn't that day come?

Repeat the texts:

Jesus said:

If the light that is in you is darkness, how great is that darkness!

Clean the inside of the cup.

You are like tombs covered with whitewash; they look well from outside, but inside they are full of dead men's bones and all kinds of filth.

Seek for yourselves a place within for rest, so that you do not become a corpse.

Disciples: On what day does the new world come?

Jesus: What you are waiting for has come, but you do not recognise it.

***

9 THE MAGIC MIRROR—THAT SHOWS YOU WHAT YOU ARE NOT LIKE

Jesus said:

You examine the face of the heaven and the earth, and you do not know what is where you are.

Look upon the Living One as long as you live.

A greater than Solomon is here.

***

Time: 9 mins.
Gear: One hand-mirror per player.
Set-up: None.

Another objection:

"But I do have a face—I see it in the mirror!"

Carefully investigate that face in your mirror.

DOES IT FIT YOU?

Is it in the right place? Or too far off?

Is it the right size? Or too small?

Is it the right way round? Or the wrong way?

Does it feel right? Or too smooth?

To make a proper face of it, one that fits, try:

bringing it slowly forward,
enlarging it as it comes,
turning it the right way round,
holding it in place here,
and feeling it again.

Total failure?

Can you find any way of putting on that face without losing it altogether?

Why not stop playing impossible tricks with your mirror, and trust it?

Let it show you where you keep that face—out there, where it's presented to other people and their cameras.

Why not use your mirror honestly, taking its message to heart?

Allow it to show you what you are *not* like.

Can you now say to that face:

"Thank God I'm not like *that!*"

"*Here,* my complexion is absolutely clear, ageless, perfect!"

"Here, in fact, is not the face of man, but the unveiled face of One who is greater than Solomon, greater than the Temple, greater than all things!"?

Repeat the texts:

Jesus said:

You examine the face of the heaven and the earth, and you do not know what is where you are.

Look upon the Living One as long as you live.

A greater than Solomon is here.

***

10 OVER THE WORLD'S EDGE

Jesus said:

Seek for yourselves a place within for rest.

Take my yoke upon you… for my yoke is easy, and my load is light.

***

Time: 6 mins.
Gear: None.
Set-up: Sit in a circle facing inwards, legs stretched out.

The world is in turmoil.

Can we 'stop it and get off'?

Or jump over its edge into a more restful spot?

Is there such a place as the world's end, where this scene borders on the kingdom of Heaven?

Let's see if we can locate it, and actually map the frontier. Start with the opposite wall, where it meets the ceiling, and work down, till you get to the face of your opposite number,
to his chest,
stomach,
legs,
feet;
then your feet,
legs,
stomach,
chest....

Outline with your finger the edge of the world,

the arc-shaped frontier between the kingdom of this world

and the kingdom of Heaven, the place of rest.

This is your yoke.

Notice how easy it is, how light the load it carries.

Isn't it always peaceful, this side of the border?

Repeat the texts:

Jesus said:

Seek for yourselves a place within for rest.

Take my yoke upon you… for my yoke is easy, and my load is light.

***

11 CLEANED OUT

Jesus said:

The kingdom of the Father is like a woman who carries a vessel full of meal and goes a long way. (The vessel sprang a leak.) The meal flowed out behind her on the way.... When she reached her house she set the vessel down and found it empty.

If you wish to be perfect, go and sell all you have.... It is easier for a camel to pass through the eye of a needle than for a rich man to enter the kingdom of God.

***

Time: 8 mins.
Gear: One card per player, about 12 in. x 12 in., with a head-shaped, head-sized hole in it.
Set-up: None.

Hold out your card at arm's length.

Note the total opacity of the card, and the total transparency of the hole.

Put the card on slowly, watching what's happening to the edges of that hole.

Put it right on.

Observe how the small *seen* emptiness becomes, without a break,

the boundless *seeing* emptiness.

Has that hole ceased to be visibly empty, now it has no boundaries? By wearing it, do you fill it?

If so, at exactly what point did the hole get filled?

Keeping the card on, compare what's happened to your card with what's happened to the other cards—filled with those funny faces.

Instead of the card, try using your hands.

Hold them out at shoulder height, about 18 inches apart, and watch the space between them grow
to infinity
as you bring them slowly up to and past you.

Game 11 Cleaned Out

A clean sweep!

Rich or poor, you can't take it with you.

You can't even have it *now!*

On the way home you are cleaned out.

Repeat the texts:

Jesus said:

The kingdom of the Father is like a woman who carries a vessel full of meal and goes a long way. (The vessel sprang a leak.) The meal flowed out behind her on the way.... When she reached her house she set the vessel down and found it empty.

If you wish to be perfect, go and sell all you have.... It is easier for a camel to pass through the eye of a needle than for a rich man to enter the kingdom of God.

***

12 THE HEAD OF THE CHURCH

Jesus said:

Where two or three are gathered together in My name, there I AM in the midst.

***

Minimum no. of players: 4.
Time: 8 mins.
Gear: None.
Set-up: Stand in a close circle, embracing your neighbours, looking down at the floor. More than 12 players should form 2 circles.

Note: If you intend, after this play-session, to go on to some games from Parts 2 or 3, do so now, and leave this game till the end. It is a good one to finish on—a good-bye (God be with you) which shows there can be no parting.

Silence, for a minute, or so.

Here is a circular temple—with floor, columns, walls and no roof—a temple wide open to wind and cloudless sky: sky infinite and indivisible.

St Paul says:

"You are the temple of God, and the Spirit of God dwells in you."

Here is a many-limbed, many-trunked body—with one Head, absolutely clear.

St Paul says:

"He is before all things, and by him all things consist, and he is the Head of the body, the Church."

Here are a few friends gathered together, not in their own names, but in the name that is above every name, My name,

the I AM in the midst.

Silence.

Repeat the text:

Jesus said:

Where two or three are gathered together in My name, there I AM in the midst.

***

EVALUATION

*A*t the end of the session, if the players are new to the games, they may be invited to answer in writing (without necessarily giving their names) the following questions. Their replies may help you, and other Leaders, in the conduct of further sessions.

(1) Which of the games made their point most forcibly, were the most revealing?

(2) Which do you recall as having little impact?

(3) Which, if any, put you off?

(4) What suggestions can you make for the improvement of future sessions?

(5) Do you consider that what we have been going into is worth continuing with, till this kind of attention proves natural and effortless?

(6) If so, which games or exercises seem most suitable for unobtrusive everyday use?

(7) Could, for example, the SINGLE EYE, and YOUR NEIGHBOUR AS YOURSELF (face-to-no-face, but without the paper bag) be practised, with benefit and not too much difficulty, in the street, at work, in the home?

(8) Do you feel that periodical meetings, like the one we have just had, would be worth while?

(9) Can you see any obstacle to your sharing, with anyone who is sufficiently interested, what you have discovered today?

PART 2

DEVELOPED GAMES

These rather more elaborate games are for choosing from on each occasion, as time allows and players' interests indicate. They can, of course, be steadily worked through—at some risk of indigestion.

It's *reading about* them instead of *doing* them that's the real trouble. Eating the menu instead of the dinner gives no taste of what's on offer.

Lacking partners is no excuse. With suitable modifications and cuts (which will readily occur to anyone sufficiently interested) most of the following games can be enjoyed on your own.

13 SORT YOURSELF OUT

Jesus said:

My kingdom does not belong to this world.

Unless a man is born again he cannot see the kingdom of God.
Flesh can only give birth to flesh; it is spirit that gives birth to spirit.
The wind blows where it wills; you hear the sound of it, but you do not know where it comes from, or where it is going. So with everyone who is born from spirit.

What I now seem to be, that am I not.
And so speak I, separating off the manhood.

***

Minimum no. of players: 4.
Time: 15 mins.
Gear: Self-adhesive spots, in 5 colours.
Set-up: Stand around, in silence, eyes closed.

"You are not in the flesh", says St Paul, "but in the spirit."

He points out that there are many kinds of flesh, of bodies, but only one spirit, in which there is neither Jew nor Greek, male nor female, slave nor freeman.

As spirit, one is unclassifiable; one belongs to no categories whatever.

Go round putting a coloured sticker on the forehead of each player, while all have their eyes closed. If you can, put 2 (differently coloured) stickers, or no sticker at all, on one or two players, without their realising it.

Now the rules of this game are that you mayn't look in any reflecting surface, or take off your sticker, or say anything; otherwise, you may act as you please.

You have now been classified.

When I clap my hands, open your eyes,
and all the reds get together near the door,
all the blues near the window,
all the yellows near the fireplace, etc.

Those of you who have played this game before should go slow, and give the others their chance.

Having clapped your hands, wait for something to happen.

Sort yourselves out somehow, keeping to the rules.

Game 13 Sort Yourself Out

Sooner or later, someone realises that he can silently guide others to their right stations, and in turn get guided himself. If there are some players who haven't been properly colour-coded, they are likely to find themselves pushed around from group to group, and to end in the middle, unclassifiable.

If any of you are still not certain which group you belong to—if any—why not come and stand here in the middle?

Now you are all, more or less, sorted out, what is the lesson of our game?

Get answers from the players, before checking against the following list.

(1) In myself, as 1st-person spirit, I am spotless, colourless, boundless as the wind, in no category.

(2) Yet all the categories of the flesh, of 3rd persons—red, blue, yellow, etc.—are in me, presented to me here.

(3) Only for these others, as the 3rd-person flesh they see, am I in any category, and even now I only have their word for it.

(4) Being born as spirit is seeing that the kingdom of God, which is right here, doesn't belong to the world, though the world belongs to it.

Repeat the texts:

Jesus said:

My kingdom does not belong to this world.

Unless a man is born again he cannot see the kingdom of God.

Flesh can only give birth to flesh; it is spirit that gives birth to spirit.

The wind blows where it wills; you hear the sound of it, but you do not know where it comes from, or where it is going. So with everyone who is born from spirit.

What I now seem to be, that am I not.

And so speak I, separating off the manhood.

***

14 HOW TO LIGHT UP THE WORLD

Jesus said:

I AM the light of the world.

You are the light of the world.
When a lamp is lit it is not put under a basin but on the lamp-stand where it gives light to everyone in the house.

His disciples said:
Show us the place where you are,
for it is necessary for us to seek it.

He said to them:
There is light within a light-man
and it illuminates the whole world.
If it does not illuminate it—darkness.

***

Minimum no. of players: 4.
Time: 7 mins.
Gear: None.
Set-up: Sit on the floor in compact groups of 4—A, B, C, D.

A and C look steadily across at each other, B and D likewise.

All 4 of you are now doing the same thing—looking at your opposite number.

At least, that's *my* story.

Is it yours?

Going by what's given now, is your group a foursome, or a threesome?

Four 'basins', or three basins and one 'lamp'?

Is there one kind of 'looking' going on, in four places, or *two* utterly different sorts?
If two, which is the real one?

'I look', 'they look'; 'I see', 'they see'—the same word must mean the same thing!

Notice how words trick us:

You say: "I *see* the person opposite, and he *sees* me, and the other two *see* each other."

As though there were no difference between these operations!

Observe carefully: is the true seeing going on where there are eyes, or where there are no eyes?

Game 14 Light up the World

Look round the room, and out of the window.

Locate the 'light of the world'.

Notice how different it is from all it shines on.

Repeat the texts:

Jesus said:

I AM the light of the world.

You are the light of the world.
When a lamp is lit it is not put under a basin but on the lamp-stand where it gives light to everyone in the house.

His disciples said:
Show us the place where you are,
for it is necessary for us to seek it.

He said to them:
There is light within a light-man
and it illuminates the whole world.
If it does not illuminate it—darkness.

***

15 TREASURE HUNT

Jesus said:

The kingdom of Heaven is like a man who has in his field a treasure which is hidden, of which he knows nothing.

Seek the treasure which does not perish, which abides where no moth enters to eat and worms do not destroy.

Where your treasure is, there your heart will be also.

∗∗

Time: 17 mins.
Gear: Drawing materials.
Set-up: Sit in a circle on the floor, *facing outwards,* with a drawing pad or card on the floor between your knees.

Draw a sketch-map of your 'field'—*of what you actually see*—starting with your feet at the top of the map.

Add an arrow to show the direction of the treasure.

When you have all finished, get up—leaving the maps in position on the floor—and stand aside.

Notice how, though the maps are of different fields, their arrows point
to the *one* imperishable treasure,
to the *one* no-head of all those headless bodies,
to the *one* kingdom within.

What a place to keep your treasure—'closer than breathing, nearer than hands and feet'!

Repeat the texts:

Jesus said:

The kingdom of Heaven is like a man who has in his field a treasure which is hidden, of which he knows nothing.

Seek the treasure which does not perish, which abides where no moth enters to eat and worms do not destroy.

Where your treasure is, there your heart will be also.

***

16 THE EMPEROR, THE DRUNK-ARD, THE TEAPOT, AND THE GHOST

Jesus said:

I stood in the midst of the world
and I appeared to them in the flesh.

I found them all drunk.
They are blind in their hearts
and do not see that they came empty into the world.

***

Minimum number of players: 6. Time: 20 mins.

Gear: Four similar chairs. A large teapot or similar vessel. A pile of heavy books, or other substantial objects, to put on a chair to raise the teapot about 2' 6", to eye-level. A (paper) hat. Two masks, one lunatic and the other ghastly: they can be home-made, but must be hidden from the players till they are used. An open-ended paper bag, about 12" x 12".

Set-up: Sit in a horse-shoe, with the 4 chairs lined up at the open end.
On chair 1 put the hat, on chair 2 the lunatic mask in its box, on chair 3 the teapot on its pedestal. Chair 4 stays empty.

Note: More than in simpler games, the Leader may have to vary the details as he goes along, to fit players' needs and responses. Much will depend on whether they are new to the game. After some experience, he will discover how far he can improvise without losing sight of the simple message of our quotation.

Game 16 Drunk

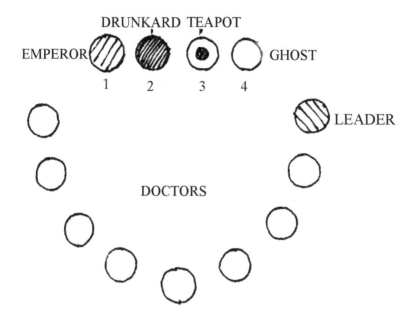

1 DRUNK

Is anyone drunk here?

Or is there a madman present?

I mean the sort that thinks he's a teapot, or Napoleon, or whatever?

Well, since you are all perfectly sane and sober, one of you will have to *pretend* to be crazy-drunk.

A volunteer, please.

Instruct the volunteer to sit in chair 2, and close his eyes while you take the lunatic mask from its box and put it on him.

Here's our crazy man, with teapot alongside.
Now who will play the part of Napoleon?

Instruct the volunteer to go to chair 1, put the hat on sideways, sit down, and place his hand on his stomach.

The rest of you are a panel of doctors—remarkably attentive and candid ones. Here is your patient, for diagnosis.

Sometimes he says he's the Emperor Napoleon there.
Sometimes he gets himself confused with that teapot.
A sad case! Is it the drink?
Whatever could possess him—to mix up such *unlike* things as those occupying chairs 1, 2, and 3?
Observe carefully the striking differences between your patient and Napoleon. And now the still more striking differences between him and that teapot.

All the same—to be fair—he does have some excuse: there are resemblances. Observe how, for instance, like Napoleon, he has this large hairy globe at the top of his body, with holes in roughly the same places. Again observe how, like the teapot, he is well-rounded,
and has a kind of spout,
and is coloured all over and perfectly opaque,
and has well-defined limits showing up against a background.

The truth is that he could be a lot crazier, or still more drunk, and not just confuse one of these things with another, but with *nothing*,
with empty space itself.
For example, he could insist that there's somebody sitting on chair 4.
Fortunately, your patient isn't as fuddled as that!
At least he doesn't, like Macbeth at the dinner party, see a Banquo in that empty seat.

To show what *that* would be like, will somebody play Banquo.

The volunteer is asked to close his eyes while you take the ghastly mask out of its box and put it on him where he sits. You then turn to the others:

Sure enough, your patient gets mixed up with Napoleon
—patient change places with Napoleon—
but notice, all of you, how *little* this alters the scene.
But if, instead, he were to see Banquo in that empty seat
—Banquo sit there—
notice how much that would alter the scene.

Your patient could indeed be worse than he is.

Let's see what we've got now in our 4 chairs.

Are all fully occupied—with drunkard, Emperor, teapot, and ghost, in that order?

Admittedly, for a ghost, Banquo looks solid enough, and as much all there as Napoleon or the patient.

Are we all agreed about that?

All of us?

Now that's settled, go back to your place, Banquo, keeping your mask on.

2 MORE DRUNK

Banquo starts to go back, but suddenly you stop him.

Just a moment, Banquo!
Everyone—that includes you—has just agreed there was a person, all present and correct, in chair 4.
Were you being truthful?

Well, let's check up.

Standing over here, can you swear there's nobody in chair 4 now?
Let's make quite sure.
Come right up to chair 4 with me and look closely.
Still no-one there?

Now turn right round and sit down, attend to what you find, and, looking me straight in the eye, tell me:
Is a person sitting in chair 4 now?
Is Banquo here? Or his ghost?
If so, is he fair or dark, old or young-looking, brown or pink or grey or green?
Is he horrible or beautiful?

Or just absent, a missing person?

Well, to clinch it, I want you, Banquo, to stay in chair 4 and get into this paper bag—this time with the teapot instead of the face—while I ask you some more questions. Answer so we can all hear.

Help Banquo to fit his (masked) face into one end of the bag and the teapot into the other, then proceed:

(1) Can you now find even the ghost of a thing in chair 4, confronting that very substantial thing in chair 3?

(2) Where in the bag are colour? Shape? Opacity? Limits?

(3) What remains at your end?

(4) Have you, most of your adult life, been suffering from chronic DT's, and habitually seeing things that aren't present?

(5) Haunting *yourself*—with imaginary shapes?

(6) Didn't you come empty and sober, mask-less and unhaunted, into the world, and aren't you just the same now?

(7) So you admit to having been, much of the time, even more sozzled than our patient?

(8) Are you now, at least for the moment, sober?

All right, come out of the bag.

To find Banquo, you must keep your distance—like this:

Remove Banquo's mask, show it to him, and send him back to his place.

3 ALL DRUNK

Is there any doctor here who still feels superior to the patient?

Anyone who doesn't confess, for instance, to regularly counting one more person round the dinner table than are actually present?

If so, would you, too, like to sit in chair 4 and go into the matter with the teapot?

One or two more players may be bagged.

So our panel of doctors admit to being even more confused than the patient, though we are now—it seems—coming to our senses.

To help us all, including Napoleon and the patient himself, to sober up, here's a final dose of simple attention:

(1) Stretch out your arm and point to the teapot, and simultaneously (using the other hand) to your own face. Are you like that?

(2) Now point simultaneously to the patient's face and to your own face.

Aren't you *just as different* from that, as you were from the teapot?

(3) Now point, as before, to the emptiness—the absence of Banquo's face—in chair 4.

And see if *that* isn't more like you now.

Repeat the texts:

Jesus said:

I stood in the midst of the world
and I appeared to them in the flesh.

I found them all drunk.

They are blind in their hearts
and do not see that they came empty into the world.

***

17 YOUR SIDE OF EVERY STORY

Jesus said:

Come into being as you pass away.

Whoever does not give up all he has cannot be my disciple.

How blest are they that know they are poor;
the kingdom of Heaven is theirs.

In my Father's house are many mansions.

***

Time: 10 mins.
Gear: None.
Set-up: None.

Looking carefully at your hand, answer—silently—these questions:

(1) How could you see its colour, if you were coloured?

(2) How could you be open to its shape, if you had shape?

(3) How could you take on all that complexity, except by being quite simple?

(4) How could that hand now display its boundaries, except in your boundlessness?

(5) How could it be something for you, while you are something for yourself?

(6) How could you hear its sound (as you snap your fingers), if that sound didn't plop into the pool of your silence?

(7) How could you feel pain there (as you press a fingernail into your thumb), except against a background of no-pain?

(8) How could its movements display themselves (as you wiggle your fingers), unless in contrast to your stillness?

(9) How could you feel tension there (as you make a fist), if you were like that?

(10) How could those fingers feel (as they move against one another), if you, too, were feeling?

Game 17 Your Side of Every Story

Is it true that, though indivisible and simple, the emptiness where you are has endless aspects—a special absence corresponding to each presence, fitting it like a glove?

You name it: doesn't the kingdom within provide perfect accommodation—a special mansion or capacity—for just that thing?

Look at that brightly coloured object
(say, a red scarf: anything will do):

What's your side of the red?

Aren't you now nothing-but-red?

How could you be more reddened?

Is there anything you can't make room for—giving it exactly the housing it needs—with the result that you become it?

As this infinitely elastic and many-sided capacity, what do you lack?

Yield—and see what the yield is!

Repeat the texts:

Jesus said:

Come into being as you pass away.

Whoever does not give up all he has cannot be my disciple.

How blest are they that know they are poor;
the kingdom of Heaven is theirs.

In my Father's house are many mansions.

***

18 CONFIDENCE TRICKS

The disciples asked:
When will you be visible to us and when
shall we see you?
Jesus replied:
When you are stripped and are not
ashamed.

St. Paul said:
'Whenever he turns to the Lord the veil
is removed.'
Now the Lord of whom this passage speaks
is the Spirit....
And because there is for us no veil over
the face, we all reflect as in a mirror
the splendour of the Lord;
thus we are transformed.

***

Time: 20 mins.

Gear: Writing materials.
In readiness for this game, make up 6 separate paper cut-outs like the pictures below, but big enough for the whole group to see the words clearly. If the group is small (say, 10 or less) the cut-outs aren't necessary: the pictures will do.

Set-up: Sit in a horse-shoe. The Leader, armed with the cut-outs (their blank sides to the players, who must have no preview), is at the open end of the horse-shoe.

Game 18 Confidence Tricks

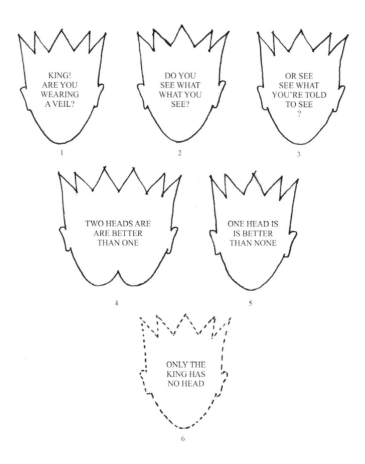

Read out the following version of the fairy story made famous by Hans Christian Anderson:

There was once a king who was visited by some confidence-tricksters who claimed they were tailors, and could make him a magic suit of clothes—clothes which wise men could see were magnificent, but fools couldn't see at all.

The king having agreed, the swindlers pretended to cut and stitch away till at last the suit was ready. Afraid of being thought a fool, the king went into raptures about his new clothes, and so did the queen and the whole court—for the same reason.

On the day of the big parade all the people cheered the royal turn-out—all except one small boy who *hadn't been told what he was supposed to see.*

"Look at the king!" he yelled. "He's stark naked!"

Let's complete the story:

The small boy was taken off to the palace and given the post of Tester of the Royal Brains.

Let me try out on you a few of the tests he subjected the foolish king to:

Test 1: Display cut-out no. 1 for a few seconds, then carefully hide it. (If the group is small, cut-outs aren't essential. You can go round the horse-shoe showing players picture 1 on the previous page, having covered the other 5 with paper.)

Write down the number of the test, and against it the words you saw. Write them in one line. Don't try to reproduce their arrangement in the head-pattern.

Test 2: Repeat with cut-out no. 2.

Test 3: Repeat with cut-out no. 3.

Test 4: Swindlers come to court and try to persuade your majesty that—on the principle that *two* royal heads are better than one—you have a *pair* of them on your shoulders.

Would you believe them? Write down Yes, or No.

Test 5: Others—in fact, *all* your subjects—insist you have *one* head on your shoulders.

Look and see: are they any nearer the truth than the first lot of confidence-tricksters? Write down Yes or No.

Test 6: At last a boy comes along and says: "Your majesty: a crown and royal robes don't make a king. To find him, look for the *only* one who has neither crown nor anything to put it on."

Is the boy a swindler, too? Write Yes, or No.

Let's look again at the choice confronting his majesty:

Test 7: Display cut-out no. 4, then hide it.

Write down the words you saw.

Test 8: Repeat with cut-out no. 5.

Test 9: Repeat with cut-out no. 6.

Test 10: Repeat with cut-outs nos. 2 and 3, displayed together.

Assessment: Each player reads out, in turn, exactly what he has written, in answer to the 10 royal tests.

***

19a HOW TO SEE GOD

Jesus said:

Why do you call me good?
There is none good but one: that is God.

The Father is in me.

When you see the one who was not born of woman.... he is your Father.

Blessed are the pure in heart,
for they shall see God.

The time is coming when....
I shall plainly show you the Father.

***

Time: 8 mins.
Gear: None.
Set-up: Get into pairs.

We think that it is easy to see a man, but hard to see God; easy to see a hand, a flower, a chair, but hard to see its *origin*. Let's test this.

Examine very carefully your neighbour's face, at a distance of about 10".

Notice how, at this very moment, only a tiny area—
a wrinkle, a pore, a hair or two
—stands out sharp and clear,
and how hazy it becomes when you shift to another.

Go on scanning that scene.

How many days, months, years, would it take to attend to every detail in turn, so that at last you could say you had clearly *seen* that face—had taken in the lot?

Would it obligingly stay the same, awaiting the end of your survey?

Could you hope to keep pace with its changing?

Could you ever see it with complete objectivity, as all others might do?

Aren't your ever-changing viewpoint, the pattern of your scanning, indeed all your impressions, at least as much to do with you as with him?

In short, can you ever do more than *glimpse* your

neighbour?

Now, still looking at his face, compare it with yours—
with your no-face, the kingdom within,
'the one who was not born of woman'.

Seeing *this*, don't you see it all-at-once, free of time,
perfectly (with or without your glasses),
as it always was and will be,
exactly as Jesus saw it 2000 years ago,
exactly as every one of its observers—past, present, future—sees it?

What is here to uncover, to differ about, to get to know better?

To see this at all is to see it to perfection.

Only God can be truly seen because only God is truly simple.

And who could it be that is now seeing God here, but himself?

Repeat the texts:

Jesus said:

Why do you call me good?

There is none good but one: that is God.

The Father is in me.

When you see the one who was not born of woman.... he is your Father.

Blessed are the pure in heart,
for they shall see God.

The time is coming when....
I shall plainly show you the Father.

***

19b HOW TO HEAR GOD

Time: 16 mins.

Gear: Preferably a loud gong or bell, but any musical instrument will do.

Set-up: Sit in a circle, holding hands.

Note: If alone, you will have to improvise. You could, for instance, compare the talking face of a television actor with the viewer's silent no-face.

1 JESUS SAID—

None of the so-called saying of Jesus is authentic beyond doubt. Besides, even if we could be sure of the words, how could we know all the shades of meaning they held for *him*—to say nothing of *his hearers* in all their variety? And how could we catch, at this range, his tone of voice?

There is one exception.

Can you guess which it is?

Here are 10 clues to the riddle:

(1) Its genuineness cannot be doubted.

(2) It is exact. No gospel-maker or translator or theologian ever twisted it.

(3) It is deep, penetrating to the very heart.

(4) It is changeless, and means for us just what it meant for him.

(5) It is so simple—so transparent that the stupidest can take it in, and the cleverest cannot complicate it.

(6) It is unforgettable.

(7) It is timeless, eternal.

(8) It is universally agreed, and bridges the gaps between all Christian sects. There can be no argument, no two opinions, about it.

(9) It is in constant use.

(10) A well-known Christian sect bases its religious practice upon it.

Well, what is it?

Pay no attention to spoken answers, but wait until a silence of, say, half a minute has elapsed. Then:

That's right! You've got it.

Jesus said:

Another silence

2 HEARING SILENCE

Go on holding hands, but close your eyes, and listen.

Listen, first, *for* the sound I'm going to make.

While waiting, hear it's absence.

Notice how *audible* that absence is.

Only *hearing* can tell you there's nothing to hear: smell and taste certainly can't.

Now make the sound—preferably a loud clang that gradually tails off, like the sound of a gong.

When it's quite gone, proceed:

Did you notice how your hearing the sound shaded off into your hearing its *absence,* the silence it occurs in, and occurs to?

Let's try it again.

Repeat the experiment..........

Keep your eyes closed and attend carefully to the sounds I'm making now.

Notice how it takes time to experience this sentence. how... this... word.. replaces... those... that... went... before,

...how... this word-pattern... cannot... be... received... all at once.

By the time you get to the end of it the beginning is a memory, already fading and unreliable.

Not only is it impossible to take in the whole of this sentence at once, ...but... even... the... part... you... are... distinctly... hearing is hard to... grasp, with all its subtle undertones and overtones,... in such a way that you could recall it or reproduce it.

If all these difficulties are true of a sentence, how much more true they are of a lecture, a symphony, the sermons of Jesus.

We say we *hear* a whole sentence, a piece of music, a man's teaching, but isn't this hearing, after all, mostly deafness?

But now listen to the voice, not of man, but of God, to the voice of the universal Christ:

SILENCE

Isn't this the perfection of speaking and hearing,
for here the speaking *is* the hearing,
and the Speaker is the Hearer,
and the message is given all-at-once, involving no memory

or time,
and is so clear that to get it at all is to get all of it.

3 THE STILL VOICE

While listening to the words I'm going to read, listen also
to the Quiet,
to the Stillness from which they arise,
which underlies them,
into which they fall back.

Open your eyes.

While seeing this very human face of mine,
and hearing this very human voice of mine,
see and hear, your side of both,
the expressionless Face,
the still Voice,
of God himself:

A great and strong wind rent the mountains
and broke in pieces the rocks before the Lord,
but the Lord was not in the wind.
And after the wind an earthquake,
but the Lord was not in the earthquake.
And after the earthquake a fire,
but the Lord was not in the fire.
And after the fire a still small voice.

And when Elijah heard it
he wrapped his face in his mantle, and went out.

Only God is perfectly audible because only God is perfectly simple.

Who could it be that is now listening to God, right where you are, but God himself?

Who could it be that is simultaneously seeing and hearing God, right where you are, but God himself?

Aren't his hearing and seeing identical?

>Be still, and know that I AM God.

***

20 THE PRINCE, THE SERPENT, AND THE PEARL

Jesus said:

Get behind me, Satan.

The prince of this world comes, and has nothing in me.

Seek first the kingdom of God…..
and all these things shall be added.

***

Time: 20 mins.
Gear: None.
Set-Up: None.

Here (with the less important parts cut out) is 'The Hymn of the Pearl', from the 3rd century *Acts of Thomas:*

When I was a little child,
And dwelling in the kingdom of my Father's house....
My parents, having equipped me, sent me forth....
And they made a compact with me,
And wrote it in my heart that it should not be forgotten:
"If you go down to Egypt,
And bring the One Pearl,
Which is in the midst of the sea
Hard by the loud-breathing Serpent....
You shall be heir in our kingdom."

(The Prince, arrived in Egypt, puts on the clothes of the Egyptians and eats their food and becomes drugged; and so he forgets who he is. The King, hearing of this, sends a letter to remind him.)

I remembered that I was a son of kings
And my freedom longed for its own nature.
I remembered the Pearl,
For which I had been sent to Egypt,
And I began to charm him,
The terrible loud-breathing Serpent....
At this point we break off the story to look at the Prince's situation.

20 The Prince, The Serpent and the Pearl

How can he get past the Serpent to the Pearl?
It can be done.

See if you can find the way.

Show the players the picture-puzzle below, of the Serpent and the Pearl. Give them a minute or two to solve the puzzle—each for himself—in silence.

We continue with our story, which we shall now expand and up-date:—

The Prince tries out various methods of dealing with the Serpent.

First, he *fights* him, attempting to kill the beast or at least to knock him out. This suits the Serpent because he has limitless powers of regeneration, and as soon as one claw or head is hacked off he grows two more. Meanwhile, his Pearl is quite safe.

At last the Prince, realising how futile is the method of direct attack, tries subtler ways.

He *studies* the Serpent, makes friends with him, takes many photographs of his scaly coils, in order to discover—one day—the best way of getting past him to the Pearl. But again, the Serpent is delighted, and never stops showing off for the Prince's benefit. In fact, under assumed names, he runs printing presses which turn out at least one book every day, entitled *Get to know your Serpent,* or something like that—just to be helpful.

But the Prince eventually sees through the trick, declines to become a life-long student of Serpent ways (the more you know them the more there is to know) and turns to more promising ways of getting the Pearl.

20 The Prince, The Serpent and the Pearl

The Serpent has a great variety to offer.

For instance, he promises the Prince that as soon as he has cleaned up the yard a little, and sorted out a small pile of Serpent's garbage, he will reward him with the Pearl. But the Serpent keeps on finding new garbage cans and (when the Prince's back is turned) emptying them onto the pile, which grows behind even faster than the Prince reduces it in front.

Or the Serpent may confidentially admit to the Prince that he doesn't, after all, command the path to the Pearl: the real route lies through remote and romantic lands (where people's eyes are a different shape), though even there it is deceptively sign-posted.

Or the Serpent may turn his collar round and, posing as some kind of game-keeper, warn the Prince that he needs a special licence to come Pearl-fishing. The penalty for poaching may no longer be burning-at-the-stake but it is still severe.

Or the Serpent may (speaking the truth for once) point out that the One Pearl is in fact the plainest and dullest jewel imaginable, a no-jewel and (in a sense) something of a hoax; and offer the Prince instead all manner of coloured and faceted and irridescent jewellery—beautiful stuff really worth going for.

Whatever else happens, the Serpent will certainly try to prove to the Prince that he is Egyptian through and through, born and bred, and that he has no business with foreign royalty and their missing jewels. All this is fantasy, as all right-minded Egyptians know.

And so on and on. Anything to put the Prince off the Pearl. The Serpent's repertoire of diversions is endless.

We have, of course, been making our own additions to the ancient tale. What happened in that tale was that the Prince, happily, was *not* diverted, but grasped the Pearl while its guardian was dozing—for even Serpents drop off sometimes.

And I snatched away the Pearl,
And turned to go back to my Father's house.
And their dirty and unclean clothes
I stripped off, and left them in their country,
And I took my way straight to come
To the Light of our Home.

But how did the Prince actually *reach* the Pearl?

Let's examine our picture-puzzle again. But first, here's a clue:
ONLY THE PRINCE CAN GET THE PEARL.
Looking carefully around, he actually *sees* that whereas there is always some distance, a visible division, between all others and the Pearl, between himself and the Pearl is none whatever. IT IS IN HIM. IT IS HIM. And all the Serpent's pretence of guarding his treasure was mere play-acting.

Show the picture again, and if necessary point out the 2 kinds of 'seeing' that are going on in the room—those faces-

20 The Prince, The Serpent and the Pearl

to–Pearl with distance between, and this no-face-to Pearl with no distance between. Continue reading:

Did you notice that the Prince didn't *get past* the Serpent: how, attending to the Pearl, he's already past, and the Serpent's left behind at his back, powerless to interfere?

But the monster is still around. When the Prince gains the Pearl he doesn't lose the Serpent.

The difference is that his sting is drawn, his bluff is called, he's seen for what he is. From now on, the Prince holds (in the shape of the Pearl) a bright torch which shows up all that confusion of shiny scales and writhing limbs far more clearly than before.

Even so, the Serpent can still lash out. He doesn't grow into a pussycat overnight. He can put on a special act of fury when he loses his Pearl.

But he has met his Master, indeed his Origin, and knows his place.

The Prince wouldn't be without him.

Well, that's the end of the story.

What do you make of it? What are the Prince, the Serpent, and the Pearl? And what, exactly, are the tricks of the Serpent?

The players discuss. To wind up, you may offer the following suggestions:

The Prince is yourself. The Serpent is your past, your conditioned nature, your unconscious, all that seems to block the Light. The Pearl is that Light, the Light of the kingdom, discovered within.

The Serpent's tricks are for you to identify. Perhaps those which you fell for can now be seen to have had their uses.

Has the Serpent been the servant of the Pearl, all along?

Go for the Serpent, and you will never tame him nor get your Pearl.

Go bald-headed for the Pearl, and Serpent-taming will be added—as necessary.

Repeat the texts:

Jesus said:

Get behind me, Satan.

The prince of this world comes, and has nothing in me.

Seek first the kingdom of God…..
and all these things shall be added.

***

21 HOW TO SPIN THE WORLD

Jesus said:

If they ask you, "What is the sign of your Father who is within you?", say to them, "It is a movement and a rest."

∗∗∗

Time: 10 mins.
Gear: None.
Set-up: Clear a large central space for (say) four dancers: the rest stand aside waiting their turn.
Remove potentially dangerous objects, and be ready to support giddy players.

Ask for up to 4 volunteers.
Get them to stand, well apart, in the central clearing, and address them:

Hold out your arm at shoulder height and look steadily along it, at your thumb.

Without losing sight of the empty stillness at the near end of your arm, start rotating on the spot.

If you cease watching the still Hub you may be in trouble.

You may want to get things moving faster, but don't lose sight of the Immovable.

Now it's the others' turn.

Those of you who have already had your turn, compare what's happening to the room as they (3rd person) rotate, with what happened to it in your own (1st person) case.

If possible, repeat the game out-of-doors, and at night.

Who could spin the stars, the galaxies, but "the Father of lights, with whom is no variableness, neither shadow of turning"?

Repeat the text:

Jesus said:

If they ask you, "What is the sign of your Father who is within you?", say to them, "It is a movement and a rest."

***

22 FREEHAND, FOOTLOOSE

Time: 15 mins.

Gear: Drawing materials, including two cards (say, postcard size) per player.

Set-up: Section 1: None. Section 2: any place to walk in, preferably outside.

1 DRAWING FREEHAND

Draw an original abstract design on card 1, in one minute.

Finish now.

Did you succeed in drawing spontaneously? Or was it hard to free your hand from your head?

Let's try again, noticing that the hand is, in fact, unconnected to a head.

On card 1, *you* drew the pattern;
this time, on card 2, it's not *you* who draw, but that hand.

While the drawing proceeds (again, for one minute) notice how, at the near end of your arm, is no designer—nothing at all—to interfere with what that hand is getting up to.

Set it free to wander, and show you what it can do.

Regard it as a curious 5-limbed pet, cavorting in the playground of your emptiness, unpredictably.

On completion, display all the cards; in 2 rows—card 2 below its corresponding card 1.

Is there, on the whole, a difference between the 2 sets of designs?

Report, individually, on what you discovered when doing the 2 kinds of drawing.

2 WALKING FOOTLOOSE

Walk around—outside if possible,—and the rougher the terrain the better—carefully picking your way, for 2 minutes.

Now try something very different.

Be walked. Be footloose. Treat yourself to a free 2-minute ride on Shank's pony.

Just watch those feet picking their own way there, unsuperintended—*in your stillness here.*

3 WATCHING DISHES GET WASHED

Compare findings.

Which does a better job and gives you less trouble—the hand or foot that is connected to an imagined head, or one that is taken as it is given?

Game 22 Freehand Footloose

From now on, why not continue your investigation—washing dishes, driving, dressing, doing anything with hands or feet?

Read the text:

Jesus said:

If your hand or your foot troubles you, cut it off.

***

23 HOW TO LET YOURSELF GO

Jesus said:

I can of myself do nothing.

I am not myself the source of the words I speak to you: it is the Father who dwells in me doing his own work.

Do not worry about what to say. When the time comes, the words you need will be given you; for it is not you who will be speaking; it will be the Spirit of your Father speaking in you.

First seek the kingdom of God, and all the rest will come to you as well.
Take no thought for tomorrow: tomorrow will look after itself.

***

Time: 20 mins.
Gear: For sections 2 and 3, recorded or live music is helpful.
Set-up: Plenty of clear room.

1 SINGLES

For just one minute—wait till I give the signal—let yourself go, just like a little child.

Release yourself from your grown-up picture of yourself, and be empty. Take no thought for the next moment, but let it look after itself. Have no preview or intention. Behave as the spirit moves you, not as your thinking dictates.

Lying down or sitting or standing or dancing, silent or muttering or talking or singing—whatever is given, let it happen.

Let the river flow freely, *without losing sight of its still Source within.*

Let yourself go—NOW!

2 PAIRS

Get into pairs and stand facing and holding hands.

Attending to your common Source, the Father within, the Unmoving, let yourselves go,
be danced.

Neither of you leading, allow the One to act as one.

3 ALL TOGETHER

Standing in a circle facing inwards and holding hands, attend to the Stillness that's nearer than all those arms and legs, and see what they get up to.

4 PRACTICE

Have you, at least for a few, freeing moments, realised within the one Source of all spontaneity and creativity? Have you, enjoying this with others, found no others, no clashing and separate inspirations, but a single smooth pattern weaving itself?

Do you fear that, in ordinary life, access to this Source will prove very difficult, often impossible?

Or that, most of the time, such freedom would land you in trouble?

Could it *always* be better to act from one's Centre rather than from one's periphery, from 1st-person spirit rather than one's idea of 3rd-person flesh, from the kingdom of Heaven rather than from the kingdom of this world?

Attend to the Source, see what flows from it, and how it works.

Repeat the texts.

Jesus said:

I can of myself do nothing.

I am not myself the source of the words I speak to you: it is the Father who dwells in me doing his own work.

Do not worry about what to say. When the time comes, the words you need will be given you; for it is not you who will be speaking; it will be the Spirit of your Father speaking in you.

First seek the kingdom of God, and all the rest will come to you as well.
Take no thought for tomorrow: tomorrow will look after itself.

***

24 TO THE FAR COUNTRY—A REAL-LIFE ADVENTURE IN 8 PARTS

Jesus said:

There was once a man who had two sons; and the younger said to his father, "Father, give me my share of the property." So he divided his estate between them.

A few days later the younger son turned the whole of his share into cash and left home for a distant country, where he squandered it in reckless living. He had spent it all, when a severe famine fell upon that country and he began to feel the pinch. So he went and attached himself to one of the local landowners, who sent him on to his farm to mind the pigs. He would have been glad to fill his belly with the pods that the pigs were eating; and no-one gave him anything.

Then he came to his senses and said, "How many of my father's paid servants have more food than they can eat, and here am I, starving to death! I will set off and go to my father, and say to him, 'Father, I have sinned against God and against you; I am no longer fit to be called your son;

treat me as one of your hired servants.'" So he set out for his father's house.

But while he was still a long way off his father saw him, and his heart went out to him. He ran to meet him, flung his arms round him, and kissed him. The son said, "Father, I have sinned, against God and against you; I am no longer fit to be called your son." But the father said to his servants, "Quick! Fetch a robe, my best one, and put it on him; put a ring on his finger and shoes on his feet. Bring the fatted calf and kill it, and let us have a feast to celebrate the day. For this son of mine was dead and has come back to life; he was lost and is found."

***

Minimum no. of players: 6, but, with minor adjustments, any number can manage. More than 12 should form 2 wheels.
Time: 20 mins.
Gear: Hand mirrors. (Optional: A strong light beamed onto the ceiling above the players, through pieces of coloured acetate or glass manipulated by the Leader, in time to music. The ceiling needs to be light in colour.)
Set-up: Clear a space in the room, at least 13' diameter. (An ideal alternative is a quiet lawn under waving treetops and scudding clouds.) The players lie flat on their backs,

arranged like the spokes of a wheel, with heads towards the hub and eyes closed. Put a mirror at the foot of each player. (If there is to be a light-show, the room should at first be in semi-darkness.)

Note : The reading should be specially slow, with very long pauses.

Keep your eyes closed and be very still.

We are about to explore 8 stages of our life and death:

(1) the unborn,
(2) the newborn,
(3) the child claiming his heritage,
(4) the adult outward bound,
(5) the adult looking homewards,
(6) home, as a child again,
(7) born again,
(8) the unborn, undying.

This is no mere let's pretend game. We shall see how far we can live through all 8 stages now.

Be comfortable, and keep your eyes closed.

STAGE 1—THE UNBORN

This is the Father's house—immense, undivided, eternal.

SILENCE

STAGE 2—THE NEWBORN

(Optional: Project onto the ceiling, above the players' heads, weaving coloured patterns—accompanied by music which, starting from near-silence, gathers speed and volume.)

Open your eyes, and take in some of the décor of the Father's house.

Which is born now? You, or the scene?

Have you arrived in the world, or has the world arrived in you?

Anyone who likes to stick at this stage, and play the part of Stay-at-home, the elder brother, should ignore my further instructions.

(The music and the ceiling patterns fade away; the room lights up.)

STAGE 3—THE CHILD CLAIMING HIS HERITAGE

Sit up and take notice.

Look down at your inheritance, your newly acquired personal property. Distinguish and explore those special parts of the scene which can feel, and move themselves about at your command.

Try to find out where they stop, and the rest of the Father's house begins.

Pick up your mirror and find a face. Name it.

But remain immense, containing and naming and even owning these things, without *being* them.

For you are still at home in the Father's house.

If you don't want to venture out, ignore my further instructions.

STAGE 4—THE ADULT OUTWARD BOUND

Stand up and go on facing outwards from the centre of the wheel.

Hold your mirror out at arm's length,
and see your arm as a long, narrowing road, leading into the far country.

Let your attention travel very slowly along it, all the way from your shoulder to your face there.

You say: THAT'S ME!

In that case, see *what* you are now,

and see *where* you are that,
and see in *what company* you find yourself—
to find the citizens you have attached yourself to in that far country, turn the mirror a little from side to side.

So this is what you have come to.

If this is what you are really like, and you are content, don't go on to Stage 5.

STAGE 5—THE ADULT LOOKING HOMEWARDS

Go on standing and holding out your mirror at arm's length.

Let your attention travel slowly *back* along your arm, from the far end to the near.

Compare the Father's house with that country.

Where do you belong?

Which is your real home?

If you can't make up your mind, don't go on to Stage 6, but remain standing.

STAGE 6—HOME, AS A CHILD AGAIN

Sit down as you were before.

Explore those limbs and that headless trunk again, noticing that, though they are still your personal property, they are *in you:* you are not *in them,*
but at large once more in the Father's house.

Again, examine that face in your mirror, and notice that, though it is still very much *yours,* a special part of you, it isn't *you.*

Do you feel like saying: "Thank Heaven I'm not like that!"?

If that's as far as you want to go now, remain sitting.

STAGE 7—BORN AGAIN

Lie down as you were, keeping your eyes open.

(The room dims, the music and lights start up.)

Jesus said: "In truth, in very truth I tell you, unless a man is born again he cannot see the kingdom of God."

Having no personal possessions, giving up everything, disappearing altogether, all you can say is I AM empty—for all that's going on in the Father's house, now.

If you don't feel like facing death just now, ignore our final stage.

STAGE 8—THE UNBORN, UNDYING

Close your eyes.

(The music fades away.)

SILENCE

Which has died—the scene, or awareness?

Your world, or you?

"I AM," or "I contain this or that"?

"I AM," or "I am this or that"?

Don't repeat the text.

***

25 DEAR GOD

God said:

In the beginning—God.

I am the first, and I am the last.

I am that I AM.

Jesus said:

He who seeks shall not cease till he finds,
And when he finds he will be astonished,
And when he is astonished he will reign,
And when he reigns he will rest.

***

Time: 14 mins.
Gear: Writing materials. A lighted candle on a big dish or incombustible tray.
Set-up: Kneel comfortably in a circle facing outwards, head bowed, eyes shut, writing materials ready-to-hand on the floor. The candle burns at the centre: preferably it is the main source of light.

After reading the texts, silence.

The child asks the mother: "Who made the world?"

"God did, dear."

"Who made God?"

Mother may do her best to answer, but the child, apt to feel he has asked a silly question, may never ask it again.

In fact, is it a silly question, or the most serious of all questions—the one which makes most grown-up questions look trivial by comparison?

Why should there be anyone or anything at all?

Which is the more astonishing—*what* is, or *that* it is?

Which is God's outstanding achievement—his Being, or his creation?

What further problem could baffle the I AM who, unaided, has already solved the problem of his own emergence from nothing?

If you find him worshipful, for what do you adore him?

Open your eyes now, but remain kneeling.

A small boy wrote a letter:

"Dear God, it must be fun to be you......"

Game 25 Dear God

Those of you who wish to do so, write your own letters of congratulation to God—for him alone: no-one else is to see them. They can be very short.

But while those hands out there are busy writing, don't overlook their Owner, the One Writer here, the Central Stillness from which all those hand movements are proceeding.

And now you have all finished, don't overlook the One Reader here, the Single Eye, the Clearness your side of what you have written. What need to send your letters off to him, if he is the very Light you are now seeing them by?

Who is there but himself—to congratulate himself, to find himself quite incredible?

The players turn round and burn their letters at the candle, in silence.

Repeat the texts:

God said:

In the beginning—God.

I am the first, and I am the last.
I am that I AM.

Jesus said:

He who seeks shall not cease till he finds,
And when he finds he will be astonished,
And when he is astonished he will reign,
And when he reigns he will rest.

∗∗∗

26 AS IT WAS IN THE BEGINNING

Jesus said:

The heavens will fold up and the earth before you, but he who lives from the One will not see death.

You have indeed uncovered the beginning. Blessed is he who will stand in the beginning and will know the end, and will not taste death.

The Book of Common Prayer:
As it was in the beginning
Is now, and ever shall be:
World without end, Amen.

Jesus said:

Blessed is he who was before he was made man.

***

Time: 20 mins.
Gear: A portable clock, preferably with a second hand. A current calendar.
Set-up: At first, none.
Note: If you are alone, the point of Section 2 can be made clear by getting into a paper bag with the clock—clock-face to no-face.

1 AT HOME IT IS ALWAYS 00.00 O'CLOCK.

We have heard of Eternity, of a region beyond change, of the timeless.

Well, I want you to close your eyes and block your ears while I set up here in this room 2 such places.

Place the clock (on a shelf) about 4 feet from the floor, at one end of the room, and the calendar around the same height at the opposite end. Both should be as inconspicuous as possible.

Open your eyes and unblock your ears.

I have set up 2 quite definite spots we can all agree on because we can actually see them pass beyond change and time, places where time can clearly be observed to make way for the timeless.

So get up and move around, and when you come upon one or both of these time-free places, don't give the game away.

Come and whisper your discovery to me.

I will give you one clue:

If you are thoroughly grown up you will never find them.

After a minute or two, line up all the players (including any who have solved the puzzle) in single file in front of the clock.

Game 26 As it Was in the Beginning

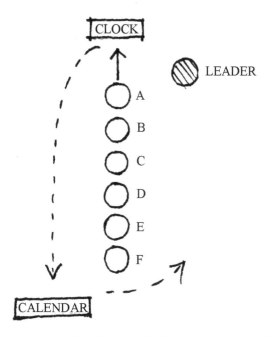

I want you (A), at the front of the queue, to tell me the time *by that clock*.

A does so.

Now move up towards the clock-face, and stop about 9 inches short of it. And tell me the time by that clock. Go only by what you see *now*.

A does so.

Now move slowly right up to the clock-face till you touch it, and tell me what the clock says *now*.

I want the time at this very moment, not the time you remember from some moments ago, the *present* time, not the *absent* time.

A, having answered, is sent off to repeat the experiment on his own, with the calendar.

The others, in turn, are given the same treatment as A, and read off the time and the date at a distance of 0" from the clock and the calendar.

Now those of you who have watches, first see what the time is *over there* on your wrist.

Then slowly bring the watch right up to you and see what the time is *here,*
for only the timepiece that is here can tell you the time that is here.

However fast or slow a clock may be, it always tells the right time at 0 inches—namely 0 hours.

Like everything else, it is *in itself* beyond time.

Time is yonder. There is then. Only here is now.

It's not enough to say: "It's 4:30p.m. 2000 miles East or West of that mantelshelf, and it isn't June 15th, 1974." When it's 4:30 on that mantelshelf it isn't June 15th on the Moon. And it certainly isn't a June afternoon *right here.*

2 THE WELL OF TIME

Place the clock, face upwards, on the floor in the middle of the room, and get the players in a close circle, looking down at it.

Look down into the well of time.

See how things moving through space mark out time, as the clock hands shift.

Listen to time ticking away in the silence here. Hear time being measured out in the timeless.

Observe the one no-face here, empty for the clock-face there, no-time here for that time to tick over in, no change or decay here, for those headless bodies down there to change and decay in. By how many minutes is each of them nearer the grave, than when we first began this game?

What's the time and what's the date, up here at the well-head?

How much older have we grown up here, where there's no *we*?

Could *this* place have a history, or *that* lack one?

Has anyone looked into time, except from Eternity?

Who is the one who is doing so here, now?

It takes 12 hours for what's down there to complete its story and start again.

It doesn't take a split second for the One up here to tell its story- a tale so brief; yet so capacious it finds room for every story.

Here, I have—I AM—all the time in the world.

But there are other dispensers of time in this well of time—ones nearer the well-head.
Breathing naturally, raise your right hand as you breathe in,
then lower it as you breathe out.
Go on doing this, noticing the differing rhythms of those hands, marking out time down there; and their unchanging container here.

Who are you?

Are you in time, or is time in you?

3 (optional) SONGS OF THE HOME WE NEVER LEFT

Sing, with accompaniment if possible:

Time, like an ever-rolling stream,
Bears all its songs away.
They fly, forgotten as a dream
Dies at the opening day.

Game 26 As it Was in the Beginning

O God, our help in ages past,

Our hope for years to come,

Our shelter from the stormy blast,

And our eternal home.

Swift to its close ebbs out life's little day;

Earth's joys grow dim, its glories pass away;

Change and decay in all around I see;

O Thou, who changest not abide with me.

Have I ever left my eternal home? Has the Changeless ever ceased to abide with me?

***

27 WHAT IS YOUR REAL NAME?

Jesus said:

I come in my Father's name.

Before Abraham was, I AM.

I AM with you always, to the end of time.

I was hungry and you gave Me food. I was thirsty and you gave Me drink. I was a stranger and you took Me into your home. I was naked and you clothed Me. I was in prison and you visited Me... When you did it to the humblest of my brothers, you did it to Me.

***

Time: 15 mins.
Gear: None.
Set-up: Stand in a close circle, facing inwards.
More than 12 players should form 2 circles.

Close your eyes.

On present evidence, what are you now?

Who are you?

What is your real name?

Though you can't say you are this or that, or anybody or anything at all, can't you still say—even more confidently than usual—I AM?

Isn't this I AM your first name, your original name?

Open your eyes and look down at those bodies, picking out the one that you call yours.

Repeat slowly, in unison:

I AM Mary/John/etc. (whatever your Christian name happens to be), listening carefully to what you hear, as you go on repeating the 3 words.

Listen to the unison of the I AM, the confusion of the separate names.

Isn't I AM your permanent name, uniting you to the whole family on earth and in Heaven, while your other names temporarily distinguish you from them?

Isn't I AM the name of what you are here, at 0 inches, while

Game 27 What is Your Real Name?

your other names belong to what you are down there, at 20 inches?

Still looking down, all point to your chests, saying, in unison:

"Before Mary (John, etc.) was", and adding "I AM", as you turn your fingers to point up to your (absence of) foreheads.

Go on repeating: "Before Mary (John, etc.) was, I AM", pointing inwards and then upwards, as before.

Now, pointing upwards only, repeat I AM, in unison, till the words end in a whisper.

"They shall see His face", says St. John the Divine, "and His name shall be written in their foreheads."

Whatever you do to anyone, you do it to one whose first or real name is I AM.

Repeat the texts:

Jesus said:

I come in my Father's name.

Before Abraham was, I AM.

I AM with you always, to the end of time.

I was hungry and you gave Me food. I was thirsty and you

gave Me drink. I was a stranger and you took Me into your home. I was naked and you clothed Me. I was in prison and you visited Me... When you did it to the humblest of my brothers, you did it to Me.

***

28 ALL CREATURES GREAT—AND SMALL?

Jesus said:

Who will draw you to the kingdom of Heaven?
The birds of the heaven
and the beasts of the earth
and the fish of the sea
—they will draw you.
And the kingdom of Heaven is within you.

Blessed is the beast which a man will eat
that the beast may become a man.

Are not sparrows two a penny?
Yet not one of them falls to the ground
without your Father.

✳✳✳

Time: 30 mins.

Gear: Any animals available and willing (or, failing that, obliged) to stay awhile—such as a dog or cat, budgerigars, guinea pigs or rabbits or white mice, the inhabitants of an aquarium, or tadpoles in a jam jar. A punnet of growing garden cress. Pot plants. If an infant of 6 months or less can put in a brief appearance, this would be useful. Scissors. Drawing materials. A mirror. Buttered biscuits.

Set-up: Sit in a circle round the menagerie.

Note: The actual menagerie, and how it behaves, will govern the details of this game.

Without warning, hold up the mirror to a player.

Repeat the experiment with 2 or 3 other players, in turn.

You noted their reactions.

Now let us repeat the experiment with the non-human members of our playshop, in turn. Observe the reactions of each one to that face in the mirror. It may be:

(1) indifference,

(2) aggression towards the intruder,

(3) attempts to make love to the stranger.

If an infant is around, repeat the experiment with him. In any case, point out that, depending on his (developmental)

Game 29 All Creatures Great and Small

age, his reactions may be:

(1) indifference,

(2) interest in that baby, and maybe a search for him behind the glass,

(3) signs of recognition of 'himself' there, and naming that face.

What is the message of our experiments so far?

What do they suggest about the way these creatures appear to themselves?

Let us now take each kind of creature here, including oneself, and try to draw it *as it could see itself*—what little there is of itself to see. In other words, let's put together a gallery of the 1st-person portraits, with the name of the sitter under each one.

Make sure the players don't start trying to draw heads.

Now let's compare drawings.

They aren't much like drawing of animals, of creatures, are they?

Again, what is their message?

Are our guests—those furry, feathered, scaly parcels of matter—as *small* as they look?

Are they shut up in those cages of skin, or are they spaced out and at large, more than roomy enough for all the 'outside' things that are now interesting them?

Isn't it *we*, sitting round the circle, who are shut up in our body-cages—or rather, think we are?

Is that bird, to its own senses, a tiny, feathered, air-borne box; or is it "an immense world of delight", closed in by *our* senses?

Is that fish swimming, or its world?

Is any creature what it looks like?

Is there anything that runs or flies or swims, or just sits around, no matter how humble, that is as *small* as man believes himself to be?

Does any creature, in its own experience, get around?

Isn't the probability that it stays still and gets the world moving?

Is it only *man* who persuades himself that he is powerless to re-arrange the whole scene, with little effort?

Aren't non-human creatures all miracle-workers, living in Wonderland?

Only that dog can say, of course, *what* he's experiencing just now—and he won't tell.

What occupies him, the smells and tastes and sounds and

shapes and colours that are coming and going in his space, are *his* business.

But the space itself, the no-thingness which contains all these doggy things, isn't doggy: it is our business too.

The space itself is everybody's and indivisible, and its other names are consciousness as capacity, the one Light, the Experiencer.

The *experience* we don't know; the Experiencer we do know, for we are that.

As we see what *we* really are now, intrinsically, don't we see what our guests are, and come to perfect identity with these and all creatures?

For check, examine the dog now, at various distances.

Doesn't he become less than canine at close range?

At very close range, less than any thing?

For further check, try looking *with* the dog (as children like doing) instead of *at* him.

Are there *two* lookers now?

Cheek to cheek or jowl, what cheeks remain, what lines of division? What's canine, what's human, what's divine?

Can't we now say, lovingly and respectfully, to all our non-human guests here: "To *be* you, all I have to do is look here"?

Is this being sloppy and sentimental?

What about Nature red in tooth and claw, the cat and the mouse, the way of the thrush with the worm,
our own life lived wholly at the expense of other lives?

Here's a punnet of garden cress—
each little green body manifestly alive and healthy, and growing as we watch, and by no means (according to recent research) insensitive to our attitude to it.

Watch me do murder with these scissors—kill these fellow-beings off by the hundred in cold blood.

Cut the cress and serve it to the players on buttered biscuits.

Raise the morsel to your lips (what lips?) very slowly, watching carefully what happens to it—how it loses shape, opacity, colour,
acquires taste,
loses even that;
how, having died as a plant, it is now resurrected as a man;
or rather, as the undying Light itself, now perfectly united to that same Light in you—
not that there was any division in that Light, anyway.
How could you *eat* what you *aren't*?

The red-in-tooth-and-claw story remains true, of course—but as the outsider's tale, the appearance.

The real or inside story isn't at all like that.

Eating is a kind of loving—when we attend.

Can we say, "Blessed is the creature which an awakened man shall eat"?

At the start of your next meal, throughout every meal, why not 'say grace' by observing what actually happens to the food on your plate?

Conceivably, a meal could do you more good if you saw it as a truly holy communion, instead of a kind of theft, the taking of another's life.

When watering your plants, why not see Who is waiting on Whom?

When gazing into the face of your favourite dog—or confronting a huge black spider or a bullock that could be a bull—don't overlook your own face, your no-face, which is also theirs, exactly.

Do you imagine that any creature great or small (not-so-small) will altogether fail to pick up your message, and not respond rather differently?

The beautiful kinship which children and 'primitives' feel towards creatures—celebrated in countless stories and customs—isn't founded so much on our common citizenship of the animal-vegetable kingdom as of the kingdom of Heaven; and in this kingdom there are no 2nd-class citizens.

We can never join them in the kingdom of Heaven by gazing soulfully into their eyes—two, or many, or none—but only by gazing mindfully out of our own absolutely single one.

Repeat the texts.

Jesus said:

Who will draw you to the kingdom of Heaven?
The birds of the heaven
and the beasts of the earth
and the fish of the sea
—they will draw you.
And the kingdom of Heaven is within you.

Blessed is the beast which a man will eat
that the beast may become a man.

Game 29 All Creatures Great and Small

Are not sparrows two a penny?
Yet not one of them falls to the ground
without your Father.

***

29a THE SECRET DOOR

Jesus said:

I AM the door.

Seek and you will find; knock and the door will be opened.

***

Time: 7 mins.
Gear: None.
Set-up: None.

Do you remember the door in the wall, leading to the enchanted garden, the panel at the back of the wardrobe opening onto the magical country of Narnia, the tunnel Alice crept through into Wonderland?

Did you have such a secret door when you were very young?

Can you find it now?

Some old rooms have a built-in secret panel, a hidey-hole for something precious, or else a hidden escape hatch in case of emergency.

This is such a room!

Go round examining all four walls carefully.

If you spot the secret door, keep it to yourself.

After a minute or so:

Stop your moving round now, and stand wherever you like, with your backs to the wall, while I give you some more information about the secret door.

(1) It is your very own secret door, which only you can spot. Others pass it by. Where they see something solid, you see an opening.

(2) When you find it, it's much bigger than you had imagined.

(3) It stands wide open—a doorway rather than a door.

(4) It gives on an Immense land, the Absolute Clear Country, the Kingdom where visibility is unlimited and every vista goes on forever—unlike the closed-in kingdom of this world where all vistas end in something, such as the opposite wall, or hills and clouds, or the coloured sky.

(5) In fact, standing in this magic doorway, you see into *both* kingdoms at once—as if you had eyes in the back of your head. Like 2-faced Janus, the Roman god of doors.

(6) And in fact your secret door stands so open that there's no trace of anyone standing in it now.

(7) In fact,—you, the one who says " I AM", not the one who says "I am somebody"—you *are* that open door now.

Repeat the texts:

Jesus said:

I AM the door

Seek and you will find; knock and the door
will be opened.

"But (you may well ask) what about the *magical* world my secret door was to lead to? The door I have found leads in one direction, to the *empty* world, and in the other to the *ordinary* world, and in neither case to Wonderland. Where are the magic and the miracles and the fun?"

Perhaps our next game will show us.

***

29b INTO THE ENCHANTED GARDEN, OR HOW TO WORK MIRACLES

Jesus said:

The kingdom of the Father is spread out
upon the earth, but men to not see it.

You could say to this sycamore tree,
"Be rooted up and re-planted in the sea",
and it would at once obey you.

When you make the two one...
if you say, "Mountain move!" it will move.

Nothing will prove impossible for you.

For men this is impossible; but everything is possible for God.

If you ask anything in My name,
I will do it.

***

Time: 20 mins.

Gear: Pieces of transparent red and blue acetate, say 3 inches x 1 foot—one of each colour per player. Two white cups or beakers. One piece of string, 3 feet long, per player.

Set-up: Adapt the game to the venue. A big house with corridors, a garden, a tree-lined pool, would be ideal. Start off in a circle, with two cups—one full of water—in the middle.

Would you say that, so far, our games have shown that, nearer to you than anything whatsoever, is God?

If you still have your doubts, it may be because you seem so powerless.

You could reasonably object:

"If the kingdom and its King are right here, why don't his subjects everywhere acknowledge the fact? Why don't all things serve and obey me? Alas, the world seems to ignore its master! No miracles happen around this person, or in this person's name."

Asked for in this person's name—in any particular name—how could they happen?

Asked for in My name—in the name of the One, the name that is above every other name—how could they fail to happen? They aren't works of the flesh (of 2nd or 3rd persons) but of the spirit (of the 1st person, singular). In the kingdom of this world they are impossible (the adult world of social fictions exists to deny them); in the secret kingdom of the Father, *which only the childlike can enter,* they go on all the while.

Let's see how naturally and effortlessly all sorts of miracles come to the One—solitary, unmoving, boundless—who is so near, who is nearness itself. And how not one of them can be performed by those others—the humans or 3rd persons—over there.

Without touching those 2 cups, or manipulating them in any way:

(1) Shift them around, so that the left one is on the right.

(2) Destroy both, then remake them.

(3) Turn them into one cup.

(4) Destroy only one of them.

(5) Turn them into 3 cups. (This may puzzle some of you.)

(6) Invert the full cup, without spilling a drop.

(7) Colour both red, then both blue.

(8) Colour one red and the other blue.

(9) Make them bigger than a man, then smaller than your thumb.

(10) Re-mould them from round to oval, from shallow to deep.

Compare results. The players who succeeded can help those who failed.

Maybe none will be able, at first, to do all 10.

These are only samples of what you, in the name of the One, can do with those cups.

Work a few more miracles on them.

Can you—as spirit or 1st person—do anything else but work miracles?

Have you ever lived anywhere but in Wonderland?

Here is an ordinary piece of string.

Turn it into elastic: Shorten it from 3 feet to 2 feet to 1 foot, to 0 feet then stretch it out again.

Carry out as many of the following as the venue allows, adapting them freely:

Instead of moving down the corridor, get the corridor on

the move. Instead of walking in the garden like the others, get it all walking in you.

See how everything—not only arms and legs, but flowers and bushes and trees and houses and hills and clouds and sun—is parading in your stillness, each thing at its own pace. Halt it all.

Start it all going again, very slowly.

Stop that bird in flight.

Set the bridge moving instead of the stream.

Command the ribbon-like road to widen for you,

the city to approach,

the doll's house to build itself up into a palace,

and turn itself inside out,

and then go back to what it was, and shrink to nothing, when you have no more use for it.

Hush the noise of traffic.

Arrive at that star in an instant.

Travel to another constellation: or rather, bring it to you.

Or rather, do nothing. It is already present!

It is the prerogative of the King alone to ennoble the least of his subjects, for any reason, or no reason.

Could you take anything—a grain of sand, a leaf, a fly, a hair, a cloud—and confer upon it a unique honour and dignity, by raising it out of neglect and oblivion to become, briefly, the centre of the world, the unique end-product of evolution, the reason for creation itself?

If any doubts remain about Who is right here, see to whom the corners of the walls, telephone poles, tree trunks and their reflections in water, are pointing.

And see for what V.I.P. that glittering gold carpet is laid down across the water, to the sun.

Have you ever lived anywhere but this Wonderland?

Is there for you any *habitable* place, which is not the kingdom of Heaven?

The kingdom's watchword is ATTENTION, which is preferring God's facts to man's fictions, and submitting to his will as expressed in the way things happen to be given now to the innocent eye.

Of course, you may say, "We have been dealing with 'trivial' and 'easy' and 'impersonal' things, and have had fun. But the serious things, life's real difficulties, remain untouched."

Are they, in fact, so trivial and easy and impersonal?

The *total* difference between all things as they are *given* in the kingdom of Heaven, and as they are *imagined* in the kingdom of this world, seems unimportant only to the citizens of the latter. What could be more important than looking to see the kind of universe one really lives in, and discovering, in fact, one has been the victim of an immense confidence trick? What could be more practical, more life-changing, than the discovery or Who is here living one's life—the life of the One who is not in the world but in whom the world is? The One who is waited upon and served by every trivial thing in the world, its King?

Each one of the trivial things we have been doing is a door so low that no adult (as such) can squeeze through it; but it gives on the kingdom of Heaven.

It's still true, of course, that life remains full of problems, of anguish, of evils which miracles seemingly cannot deal with.

Again, the answer is: ATTENTION, which is preferring God's ordering of things to man's notion of how they should be.

Some of the King's commands are easy to submit to, others hard indeed. Well, let's give in now to the innumerable 'easy' and 'trivial' ones we disobeyed, and maybe the hard and long-term ones will be less hard to take—especially if they turn out to be made up out of easy moment-to-moment ones.

And maybe we shall find that *everything* that happens to and around the children of the kingdom proves miraculous, just because it is the will of the One they really are.

Look again at your Secret door, the one that opens on the clear kingdom within.

Notice that there aren't, to be quite truthful, 3 kingdoms—the kingdom of Heaven on the near side of your door and the kingdom of this world on the far side, and somewhere or other the lost kingdom of Wonderland.

There is no kingdom of this world, of common sense, of social convenience!

What you thought was that world turns out to be, when you attend, your Lost Continent, the country of endless miracles.

Even this isn't the end of the story.

When you look again from your Secret Door, in both directions at once, isn't the 'inner' kingdom of empty space absolutely united to the 'outer' kingdom of what fills that space? So that truly there's only *one* kingdom—the kingdom of Heaven and earth or the kingdom of Heaven on earth?

Repeat the texts:

Jesus said:

The kingdom of the Father is spread out
upon the earth, but men to not see it.

Game 29b The Enchanted Garden

You could say to this sycamore tree,
"Be rooted up and re-planted in the sea",
and it would at once obey you.

When you make the two one...
if you say, "Mountain move!" it will move.

Nothing will prove impossible for you.

For men this is impossible; but everything is possible for God.

If you ask anything in My name,
I will do it.

***

30 HOW TO HEAL

Jesus said:

These people have grown gross at heart....
Otherwise, they might turn round, and I might heal them.

Proclaim the message: "The kingdom of God is upon you."
Heal the sick.

Jesus stretched out his hand, touched the leper, and said: "Be clean again."

***

Minimum no. of players: 2.
Time: 20 mins.
Gear: None.
Set-up: Get into pairs and form a double circle, the patient sitting on the floor and facing the centre, the healer kneeling at his back. Or the patient sitting in a chair and the healer standing at his back. Heavy jackets should be discarded.

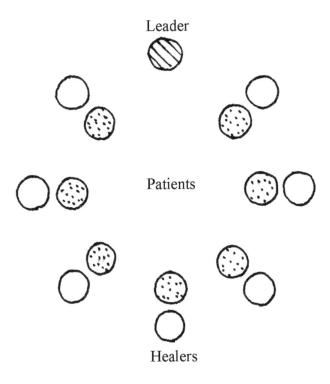

If we imagine that all the New Testament miracles really happened, and that Jesus expects us to repeat them, we are in trouble.

We are blinding ourselves to the way the biographies of religious founders invariably get written up by their devoted followers; we are miserably failing to live up to Jesus' expectations; and we could be inviting magic powers that harm us more than they help others.

It is suggested that true Christian healing gratefully uses all practicable aids, medical as well as spiritual, and leaves the upshot to God. The spiritual aspect of this healing consists in attending and submitting to him where he may be found.

This is no small adjustment.

It is the discovery that, right here, is nothing but the clear Light of his kingdom, which no shadow of sickness could ever cloud.

Young children and animals have more sense than to solidify themselves; it takes a grown-up to do that.

It is so bad for him.

If he turned round, he would melt away.

Let us try out this cure.

The one in front is the patient; the one at his back is the healer.

Here are the healer's instructions—but wait till I give the word to start:—

Slowly and with a light touch pass your hands back and forth over the patient's head and neck and shoulders, while watching the *absence* of any healer, of anybody, at the near end of those busy arms.

Start now.

And here are the patient's instructions:

Let those caressing hands draw to your notice the spot you had overlooked, the one place that is for you trouble free.

While the healing is going on, make suggestions from time to time, such as:

Just let those hands do their work spontaneously,
perhaps resting over a particular spot (is there some heat in this region?);
perhaps passing in front of the patient's face;
perhaps gently coaxing the patient's head upwards and forwards;
perhaps making no contact.

If it helps to close your eyes, do so.

If the patient finds those hands taking the tensions away, attend to the emptiness that remains.

When you feel the time has come to stop healing the patient, let your hands come to rest on his shoulders, and try putting your head immediately above his, chin on scalp. Who is now the healer, and who is the patient?

When most of the healers have finished, or after 5 minutes at most, get patients and healers to switch places and roles. Repeat the exercise.

Now all sit down in a single circle.

After this mutual laying on of hands, do you feel refreshed, relaxed, perhaps relieved of some aches and pains?

If so, good. But incidental.

What have we been up to?

We have not been trying to substitute our human will for God's, nor invoking 'healing powers',

but getting to the Source of all life—that "body full of light, having no place dark," which we see to be our true nature.

Here, what could go wrong?

Having briefly turned round and discovered, with the help of our partner, how simple (and even easy) it is to locate and rest for a little while in our Source, why should we not turn to it on our own, as often as possible?

Maybe we shall find that some of our dis-ease was attributable to the delusion that we are "gross at heart"—that we are, through and through, this ailing flesh, and have no Core of health and wholeness in us.

Maybe we shall find our human bodies growing more alive as we continue to see where their life comes from.

Let's see what difference it makes to the flesh that is always there, when we see that the spirit is always here; when we see which of these is the central Reality, and which the regional appearance.

Could it be true that profoundly to heal anybody is to demonstrate that, centrally, there's no-body to heal, but only God?

This is for testing.

Repeat the texts:

Jesus said:

These people have grown gross at heart....
Otherwise, they might turn round, and I might heal them.

Proclaim the message: "The kingdom of God is upon you." Heal the sick.

Jesus stretched out his hand, touched the leper, and said: "Be clean again."

***

31 HOW TO CAST OUT DEVILS

Jesus said:

The spirit alone gives life; the flesh is of no avail.

Woe to the flesh which hangs upon the soul!
Woe to the soul which hangs upon the flesh!

If I cast out devils by the Spirit of God,
then the kingdom of God is come to you.

***

Time: 8 mins.
Gear: Paper bags (see Game 6), one for each 2 players.
Set-up: Get into pairs. If alone, use a mirror in the bag.

Get into the bag with your partners, and answer (to yourself) these questions:

(1) Can you find any face, any flesh, any matter, at your end of the bag?

(2) Or any consciousness, any mind, any soul, any spirit, the other end?

(3) Have you been living a double lie—reading a face into this consciousness, and a consciousness into that face?

(4) How could life with your neighbour, based on such a double pretence, work out well?

Come out for a breather.

In you go again.

(5) What could be more separating, off-putting, and superstitious, than a spook peeping at you through those two little eye-windows?

(6) And what could be more re-assuring than no spook there, but a face that is only a face, a part of the décor that you could comfortably gaze at for ever, with the innocent eye of the infant?

(7) Does this mean you are robbing him of spirit, reducing him to a thing? What is spirit? Look where you are and

see if it could have limits or divisions: isn't there plenty of it for him, for every-body?

(8) How could there be *two* kinds of spirit—the angelic or divine kind at your end of the bag, immense and not yours at all; and the bottled-up or demonic kind at his end, shrunken and shut up in that tiny bone cage?

(9) Can you now say to him, "Your face is no more than your temporary appearance: I (as indivisible spirit) am no less than your everlasting Reality."?

And to all beings everywhere, "*Here,* I am you!"

Jesus prayed that we all "be perfectly one".

When the spirit seemingly divides into two sprites, one taking possession of that *seen* head there, the other of this *imagined* head here, both grow devilish, and a double exorcism is called for.

It consists in seeing that, in reality, spirit remains one and at large;

and that, though all things are in it, it is in none of them.

How could mere *things* split the no-thing, the Reality of which they are the appearances?

Madness is split consciousness, alienation, cutting oneself off.

Ultimately, all *separate* spirits are evil spirits, to be cast out in My name—the name of the Spirit of God.

From now on, you don't need a paper bag to exorcise them.

All you have to do is look to the One you found at the near end of it.

Repeat the texts:

Jesus said:

The spirit alone gives life; the flesh is of no avail.

Woe to the flesh which hangs upon the soul!
Woe to the soul which hangs upon the flesh!

If I cast out devils by the Spirit of God,
then the kingdom of God is come to you.

***

32 SUN OF MY SOUL

Jesus said:

The world cannot receive the Spirit of truth, because the world neither sees nor knows him; but you know him, because he dwells with you and is in you.

Not as the world gives, give I to you.

God's gift of the Spirit is measureless.

**

Minimum no. of players: 4, but the game is easily adapted.
Time: 10 mins.
Gear: Optional: a very bright light (pendant, standard, or table) 4 feet or less from the floor, in the middle of the room.
Set-up: Stand in a circle, well apart, facing outwards. For players new to the game, the lamp—its shadows, rather—may be too diverting. If the light is used, it should be placed at the centre of the circle, and the room should be darkened.

No doubt questions like these have occurred to some of you:

(1) Why, if God is right here, don't I enjoy 360 degree vision, and take in the whole world at once?

(2) Why don't I experience everything—or at least everything I want to?

(3) If the one Sun of consciousness is all of it shining now in me, why is it illuminating so little of the scene? Why is it reduced to a single, rather feeble, ray?

Well, here is our working model of the Sun—a single heavenly body with .... rays, poised to look into these important questions.

Stretch out your arms straight, at shoulder height, widely enough to frame the view, holding them where they just vanish from sight.

Notice how they cross your neighbours' arms, indicating the extent to which your different views of the world overlap at this time.

Now let us try to complete a 360 degree panorama, by rotating the whole circle clockwise,
slowly at first,
now rather more quickly, round and round,

like a Catherine-wheel firework.

Stop rotating now, lower your arms, and take a rest.

We are said to be body, mind, and spirit.

Let's go into this.

Raise your arms again to frame the view.

Look down at your body, and observe how *distinct* it is from your neighbours'.

Look up and out at your mind—at what's now occupying it—and observe how it *overlaps* your neighbours'.

Look in at your spirit (without turning your body, of course) and observe how it is *identical* with your neighbours'.

Looking out at the scene, with lowered arms now, consider these questions:

(1) No doubt this world of bodies and minds always gives itself to you rather grudgingly, in fragments spread over time, and never generously, all-at-once.
Is this an accident, your defect?
Or the way the world is?

(2) Examine the most prominent object that happens to confront you now.
Is it cut off from its background, from the universe, or continuous with it?
But to see it clearly, to make something of it, and certainly to name it, don't you have

to isolate it, to treat it as if it were on its own, self-contained, self-sufficient?

(3) Isn't knowledge of the world (including knowledge of your own body and mind, of your thoughts and feelings) a kind of necessary ignorance, an arbitrary carving up of what is continuous, an endless series of useful fictions?

(4) For the universe to get to work, even for it to exist as such, doesn't it need to pull itself to bits, to play hide-and-seek with itself, to pretend that most of it is missing?

(5) In short, isn't it, by its very nature, unknowable?

Now look again, not this time *down* at bodies, or *out* at mind, but *in* at spirit and consider another set of questions:

(1) Isn't the One here, in whom and for whom those body-minds exist as fragments that cannot be put together without their disappearing, himself the perfection of knowledge?

(2) Look and see for yourself.
Isn't he now completely revealed, all-at-once, clear and bright?
Revealed to himself?
Who else?

(3) See if this isn't enough.
Discover whether, *when attending to the One here,* the many there aren't presented in sufficient detail and fullness, just as they need to be at this moment,
and whether the world isn't quite sufficiently in one piece.

(4) Isn't our demand to see the world as it is *not* given, a futile attempt to give it the perfection that belongs only to its Origin?

Game 32 Sun of My Soul

Sit down now in the circle, still facing outwards:

and contrast the changing view which distinguishes you from your neighbour, with the unchanging Viewer which unites you with him absolutely;

contrast the Sun of consciousness here with what its rays are shining on over there.

Without the Sun you are benighted and lost indeed.

> Sun of my soul, thou Saviour dear,
> It is not night if thou be near.....
> Abide with me from morn till eve,
> For without thee I cannot live;
> Abide with me when night is nigh,
> For without thee I dare not die.

Finally, standing once more in the circle, arms spread wide like open gates,
attending to the opaque things you are looking *at*,
and simultaneously to the transparency you are looking *out of*,
listen to St. John's description of the New Jerusalem:

The twelve gates were twelve pearls, each gate being made from a single pearl. The streets of the city were of pure gold, like transparent glass. I saw no temple in the city; for its temple was the sovereign Lord God and the Lamb. And the city had no need of sun or moon to shine in it; for the glory of the Lord gave it light, and its lamp was the Lamb....

The gates of the city shall never be shut by day—and there will be no night.

***

33 THE FOUNTAINHEAD

Jesus said:

God is the source of my being, and from him I come.

I know him, for I am from him.

We come from the Light, the place where the Light came into existence through itself alone.

Whoever drinks the water that I shall give him shall never thirst. The water that I shall give him will be an inner spring welling up into eternal life.

I am not your master, since you drank and became drunk from the bubbling spring which I have distributed.

***

Time: 15 mins.
Gear: None.
Set-up: None.

Sit still, comfortably, eyes closed, and watch what's actually given.

Again, how many toes can you find?
How many legs?
How many fingers?
How many arms?
Trunks?
Heads?
Have you any boundaries now,
any inside distinct from outside,
any shape,
structure,
sex,
age?

Attend now to what remains quite untouched—to this core of simple Being, this Clarity.

Silence

Have thoughts and feelings already begun to invade this Clarity,
so that they seem quite central to you?

Observe them come and go.

Do you feel that you are not, alas, the Clarity at all, but this ever-shifting murk?

Game 33 The Fountainhead

First, let us take thoughts.

Think of a letter.

Where did it come from?

Did you select it from an alphabet, or did it just pop up?

From what?

Try again. Attentive to its arising, be in at the birth of another letter.

A virgin birth? Out of what womb?

Now think of a word beginning with that second letter.

Did you in imagination thumb through a dictionary to find it,
or turn it up in some memory-bank?

Or did it arrive spontaneously and unheralded out of the blue—
out of the clear wellspring of your Being?

Invite another word beginning with the same letter.

Who produced it? From where?

Did it come from a full head or an empty head or no head at all,
from a full mind or an empty mind or no mind at all,
but from Blankness?

Let's explore this Blankness.

Quickly, come up with an original joke.

Has your mind 'gone Blank'?

Yet consciousness remains. I AM isn't blanked out.

Isn't this I AM, in itself totally Blank yet totally aware, the unthinkable Fountainhead of your thoughts,
the empty No-mind which is your mind's only Source?

Now think of somebody you know well.

Don't you find your thoughts immediately *go out* to that person?

Aren't they, precisely, *about* him and not about yourself?

Don't they adhere to him and not to you, just as his colour and shape and age adhere to him?

Consider the Pole Star and the Plough.

Is your thought shut up here in a brain-box, or a mental filing-cabinet labelled 'Astronomy',
or is it not out there in the night sky?

Can you think any thought which remains quite central to you, and doesn't somehow escape into the world?

Second, let us take feelings.

What of your feelings about somebody?

Are they, like your thoughts of him, about *him,* or about yourself?

Can feelings occur centrally, right where you are, without any external reference whatever,
without flowing out and settling upon some object or other?

I'm now going to ask you to experience, if you can, certain feelings, *without linking them with anyone or anything at all.*

Feel anxiety now—
just anxiety alone, not anxiety regarding anyone or anything.

Can you do it?

Now try to feel, *by itself,* surprise.
Now compassion.
Now hate.
Now fear.
Now content.
Now love.
Well, was there any difference?

Weren't they all much the same, a sort of Blank?

Yet you weren't destroyed.

Now think of something surprising,
of someone who is in great need,
of a nasty person,
of an alarming situation....
don't your feelings flow freely out to the object,
leaving you shot of them, cool, at the Centre?

Can you feel or think anything here at the Centre except I AM?

And isn't this I AM neither a thought nor a feeling,
but their Source, upstream of mind, of all experience?

Isn't this I AM, or Consciousness, or Being, the Fountainhead of all your experience, an infinite outpouring which is never contaminated by the slightest backflow?

Isn't this marvellous Fountainhead (located provisionally where you thought your human head was, but is in fact located nowhere and everywhere)—isn't it perfectly accessible and obvious at this moment, to Itself?

Repeat the texts:

Jesus said:

God is the source of my being, and from him I come.

I know him, for I am from him.

We come from the Light, the place where the Light came into existence through itself alone.

Whoever drinks the water that I shall give him shall never thirst. The water that I shall give him will be an inner spring welling up into eternal life.

I am not your master, since you drank and became drunk from the bubbling spring which I have distributed.

***

34 THE VINE

Jesus said:

I AM the vine, and you are the branches.

From Me the all has gone forth, and to Me the all returns.

***

Minimum no. of players: 3.
Time: 9 mins.
Gear: None. Possibly drawing materials.
Set-up: Sit in a neat circle on the floor, legs outstretched, feet bunched up together in the middle.

Look carefully: are we sitting in a *circle*?

I'm not asking this question of a fly on the ceiling.

Isn't it more like a plant, a vine or a tree—the Tree of Life?—with trunk and branches and fruit,
a single fruit at the end of each branch?

Optional—Draw in outline what you see, and take your picture seriously. Note how tree-like the pattern is, and how the fruits are all at the same level.

Relying only on what's given *now*, are you one part of this tree more than the others?

Look carefully. Can you say where, on present evidence, your part ends and the others begin?

Are you clear which is the trunk of the tree? Here are 4 clues:

(1) It is the lowest part of the tree.

(2) It is central.

(3) It is about 4 times as thick as a typical branch. (You can check this by stretching out your hand and sighting a branch between thumb and forefinger, then similarly sighting the trunk.)

(4) It disappears into the ground. You could call it the

Ground of Being, which supports and nourishes and embraces the whole tree. (You can actually outline the base of the tree, where it meets the Ground, using your forefinger.)

Notice that the trunk bears no fruit, itself.

Where are you likely to find the fruits of the Spirit—in yourself, or in others?

What eventually happens to those fruits, to those branches, and indeed to the trunk?

Aren't they here for a fleeting moment, destined very soon to fall, and decay, and be re-united to their eternal Ground?

To the One who can now say, "I AM the true vine"?

***

35 THE LIVING BREAD

Jesus said:

Your whole body shall be full of light.

Take, eat: this is my body.

I AM the bread of life....
If anyone eats this bread he shall live for ever,
and the bread which I shall give is my flesh.

He who will drink from my mouth will become
as me. I too will become him and the secrets
will be revealed to him.

***

Time: 10 mins.
Gear: Anything to eat.
Set-up: If this game can be played at the start of a meal, so much the better.

Jesus recognized two versions—poles apart—of his own body:
its appearance as the body full of anatomy,
and its reality as the body full of light.

When he said, "Take, eat: this is my body", which body did he mean?

And now, whenever the miracle of the eucharist is repeated, and we believe that ordinary wheaten bread is turned into the bread of life, into his true body, which body do we mean?

Surely his light-body.

The alternative is as impossible as it is revolting.

Let us now experience this miracle,
so that, beyond any shadow of doubt, we ingest and become his body—
exactly as it was for him at the Last Supper.

Get into pairs.

A feeds B a morsel, noticing how it goes into a hole in a head,
and accordingly has no taste.

Now B feeds A, with similar results.

Now repeat both operations,
noticing this time what happens to the morsel that *doesn't*
go into a hole in a head, and accordingly has taste.
Feed each other again.

Watch for the moment when that opaque and tiny morsel becomes endless Clarity, when that thing vanishes into no-thingness,
and is lost in the indwelling Christ,
the I AM,
the Light that lights every man,
the Living Bread.

Repeat the texts:

Jesus said:

Your whole body shall be full of light.

Take, eat: this is my body.

I AM the bread of life....
If anyone eats this bread he shall live for ever,
and the bread which I shall give is my flesh.

He who will drink from my mouth will become as me. I too will become him and the secrets will be revealed to him.

✳✳✳

36 THE CROSS

Jesus said:

My task is to bear witness to the truth.
For this I was born; for this I came into the world,
and all who are not deaf to truth listen to my voice.

No man is worthy of me who does not take up his cross and follow me.

***

Time: 12 mins.
Gear: None.
Set-up: Stand well apart. If there's room, form a circle, facing inwards.

Raise your arms to shoulder height and hold them wide apart.

Look down *at* that body
from THIS.

St. Paul says:

"Our old man is crucified with him."

"I am crucified with Christ: nevertheless I live—yet not I, but Christ lives in me."

"As in Adam all die, so in Christ shall all be made alive."

Look down *at* the old man of the earth, the first Adam, the flesh, that headless mortal body.

Look down *from* the new Man from Heaven, the Head of the body, the single Eye, the one Light, the Spirit, the eternal Christ.

The very same One who 2000 years ago looked down at a body dying on a cross now looks down at your body, at the other bodies in the room.

Keep looking down.

If you can't bear the pain in your arms any longer—bear it a little longer.

See Who you obviously are.

See how limited and personal is the part you are looking down *at,* how earthbound, old, continuous with the floor, the soil.

And see how limitless and free is the part you are looking down *from;* looking down from on high, see how tall you are—above the heavens, bigger than the sky;
see how new and fresh and airy you are—as young as space itself.

There are your outstretched arms, where your heavenly nature meets your earthly, where the kingdom of the One comes down to the kingdom of the many.

Keep looking down, and try to bear the pain a little longer.

JESUS CHRIST—

Namely, JESUS the carpenter and odd-job-man of Nazareth,
joined to CHRIST the King of Heaven –

Jesus Christ saw the obvious truth of Who he really was, of Who we all are, of our dual nature:
divine above, human below: absolutely different, absolutely united.

He saw it for us, that we might see it also.

He gave himself.

He had the simplicity to see what we now see, and the courage to tell the world.

The world—religious and secular—repaid him with mockery, abuse, agony, a shameful death.

Repeat the texts:

Jesus said:

My task is to bear witness to the truth.
For this I was born; for this I came into the world,
and all who are not deaf to truth listen to my voice.

No man is worthy of me who does not take up his cross and follow me.

***

PART 3

ADDITIONAL GAMES

To break up a long session, the Leader may wish to allocate some time to an Interlude—a relaxed period for musical and other recreations, preferably held out-of-doors. Here are some suggestions.

37 ORANGES AND LEMONS

Someone volunteers to play the Debtor.

He is blindfolded, with a black hood.

All dance round him, singing this modified version of the nursery rhyme:

Oranges and lemons,
say the bells of St. Clements.

You owe us your all,
say the bells of St. Paul.

When will you pay me?
say the bells of Old Bailey.

When I grow rich,
say the bells of Shoreditch.

When will that be?
say the bells of Stepney.

I'm sure I don't know,
says the great bell of Bow.

HERE COMES A LIGHT TO LIGHT TO YOU BED
The Debtor's blindfold is snatched away.

HERE COMES A CHOPPER TO CHOP OFF YOUR HEAD
The dancers stretch out their hands towards his neck, and make chopping movements.

CHOP CHOP CHOP CHOP CHOP CHOP

Now you've nothing at all,
say the bells of St. Paul.

So now you are rich,
say the bells of Shoreditch.

They stop dancing and extend their arms in greeting towards the—now solvent—Debtor.

***

38 CURE FOR SHYNESS?

Have you ever felt like nobody—
Just a tiny speck of air
When everyone's around you
And you are just not there?
Karen (9 years)

Is anyone feeling rather shy?

Then why not play Karen?

Someone volunteers. The rest stare rudely at her, point at her, whisper remarks about her.

Whatever *their* story, how can this faceless one blush, or a 'speck of air' feel embarrassed?

***

39 MULBERRY BUSH

Using dice, a Lucky One is selected.

A Good Fairy (the Leader) grants him one wish: what would he like to be turned into?

A mulberry bush, a roaring lion, a hydrogen atom, a goblin from Mars, wide open space, or whatever?

The Lucky One states his choice.

The good Fairy tells him to drop memory and stand in the middle of the room looking straight ahead, while the rest of the fairy band dance round him singing the following threefold magic spell:

Here we go round the mulberry bush *substitute the thing he has chosen*, the mulberry bush, the mulberry bush,
Here we go round the mulberry bush,
On this cold and frosty morning.

Repeat this once or twice, then:

For all you can tell, you're a mulberry bush, a mulberry bush, a mulberry bush,
We've turned you into a mulberry bush,
On this cold and frosty morning.

Whatever a mulberry bush is to itself, is to itself, is to itself,
Whatever a mulberry bush is to itself,
Why that's what you are this morning.

Other players are invited to say what thing they would like to be turned into, undergo the threefold magic spell, and find out whether it works.

***

40 NURSERY CHAIRS

According to A. A. Milne *(When We Were Very Young)* it comes *naturally* to Christopher Robin, when he is in one chair, to be an explorer; in the second to be a roaring lion; in the third a ship a-sailing.

It is the fourth chair that presents difficulties:

Whenever I sit in a high chair
For breakfast or dinner or tea,
I *try to pretend* that it's my chair,
And that I am a baby of three.

An adaptation of this verse may be used as a grace-before-meals:

Whenever I sit in a high chair
For breakfast or dinner or tea,
I stop pretending it's my chair,
And that I'm like the others I see.

***

41 CUMBYA

This is a variation on the well known spiritual ('Cumbya' means 'Come by here'), with gestures added.

Kingdom's comin' Lord, cumbya, *Stretch out your arms*
Kingdom's comin' Lord, cumbya,
Kingdom's comin' Lord, cumbya,
O Lord, cumbya.

Not in sky, Lord, cumbya, *Point upwards*
Not in earth, Lord, cumbya, *Point outwards*
Not in sea, Lord, cumbya, *Point downwards*
O Lord, cumbya.

Not in feet, Lord, cumbya, *Point at your feet*
Not in hands, Lord, cumbya, *Point at your hands*
Not in trunks, Lord, cumbya, *Point at your trunk*
O Lord, cumbya.

Kingdom's come Lord, cumbya, *Hold out your hands*
Kingdom's come Lord, cumbya, *Look at your watch*
Kingdom's come Lord, cumbya, *Point to your face*
O Lord, cumbya.

Kingdom's come Lord, cumbya, *Go on pointing inwards*
Kingdom's come Lord, cumbya,
Kingdom's come Lord, cumbya,
O Lord, cumbya.

***

42 STORY TIME—THE WISE MEN OF GOTHAM

Once upon a time there were 7 brothers who set out to find their fortune.

In the course of their travels they came to a well. One of them, looking down the well, noticed a man there under the water. Alarmed, he got each brother to look in turn, and each saw the man in the well—and his face looked terribly familiar. Had one of them fallen in?

Each counted, and each in turn counted only 6. So they all hurriedly clambered down the well to rescue their drowning brother, leaving their hats lying on the ground above.

The water was shallow and the bottom muddy. Soon they were all so entangled into a mud-covered knot of limbs that they could hardly move. Then one of them had an idea: he began hitting here and pinching there, in order to discover what belonged to whom. Thus in the end they managed to sort themselves out and climb out of the well.

Once more they counted, and once more each found only 6 brothers. But then one of them noticed that, still lying on the ground, were 7 hats, and when they all put them on none was left over. So they went on their way, rejoicing. And wiser?

Can you find a way of dramatising this traditional tale?

A sheet over your tangled limbs could do for the mud.

***

43 FIELD SPORTS

1 TEAM GAMES

(1) The players stand in a close circle, looking downwards and noting their absolute unity at the head of the circle. (See Game 12)

(2) They close their eyes while the Leader allocates them to two equal teams (Cowboys and Indians/Angels and Devils/Cops and Robbers/etc.) by putting two kinds of simple masks on them, or marking their foreheads with finger-paint. (The *order* of the marking should be random, so that no player has a clue to his team.)

(3) The players sort themselves out into their two teams, in silence and without using mirrors. (See Game 13)

(4) They play the team game—for example: tug-of-war, football, hockey, netball.

(5) At the end of the game they get in the circle again, and re-experience their oneness, while the Leader puts these questions:

(a) You can see now that in reality (though not in appearance) you belong to neither team. It was the same while you were playing. Did this interfere with your play?

Did you still play to win?

(b) Is this game a model of—a part of—God's great game, in which the One splits up, declares war on itself, then re-unites with itself? Isn't this what the universe is all about: God's sports-day, his interior tug-of-war?

(c) Isn't it necessary to play the game—without forgetting it is a game—and to know when to stop?

2 RACES

Three-legged Race

While actually running, try seeing into your own nature, which is also your partner's. How does seeing this one (no) head affect the performance of those 3 legs?

Egg-and-spoon Race

Try keeping the egg and spoon perfectly still, and letting the world rush past them.

100-yard sprint

Try setting the scene in motion, while having a good rest yourself.

3 SWINGS AND ROUNDABOUTS

Are *you* being swung around, tossed and hurled about—or the *world*? Which feels better?

***

44 HOW GOOD IS YOUR CHINESE?

Get into pairs.

The player on the right wants to find the kingdom, but is Chinese and doesn't know a word of English. The other has 2 minutes to show him.

At the end of the 2 minutes the results are assessed, and a suitable prize—e.g., a Chinese paper hat—awarded to the best interpreter.

***

45 FULL NAME AND ADDRESS

God wants to send you a letter, by angel post, all the way from his home there (beyond the galaxies) to yours here (nearer than electrons).

Write down your *full* name and address—complete enough for the angel to find his way right up to you at this moment, yet brief enough to get on an ordinary envelope.

A prize will be awarded—say, an address book—for the postal directions voted the best.

(Did anyone conclude that the Writer of the letter is also the real addressee, and that the *human* addressee—so far from being the letter's final destination—is merely one stage of many along the angelic postman's route?)

**

46 THE KEY OF THE KINGDOM

The players sit in a square, facing inwards, and shut their eyes. The Leader fetches a bowl of scented flowers, one for each player, and sets it in the middle of the square. He then reads out the following traditional nursery rhyme:

This is the key of the kingdom:

In that kingdom is a city
In that city is a town
In that town there is a street
In the street there winds a lane
In that lane there is a yard
In that yard there is a house
In that house there is a room
In that room an empty niche
open your eyes now
And in that niche a basket
A basket of sweet flowers

Flowers in a basket
Basket in the empty niche
close your eyes now
Niche in the chamber
Chamber in the house
House in the weedy yard
Yard in the winding lane
Lane in the broad street
Street in the high town
Town in the city
City in the kingdom

This is the key of the kingdom

Of the kingdom this is the key.

The players open their eyes, and the Leader gives each a flower, in silence.

***

EPILOGUE

SCHOOLS FOR THE KINGDOM
REFERENCES

This book is a practical manual with a simple purpose, and isn't about complex issues like child-development, education, the human predicament, and the future of man. Nevertheless, the games will leave questions about these matters foremost in some players' minds. For them, this brief Epilogue may be helpful.

SCHOOLS FOR THE KINGDOM

Carlos, (2 years), at a party, pointed without hesitation to each aunt and uncle when they were named. Asked where Carlos was, he just waved his hands. Around this time, when rebuked for being a naughty boy, he didn't mind being called naughty, but protested that he was not a *boy*.

Tenniel, (5 years), asked his mother why she and his sister had heads, whereas he had none. Fingering his head, he added, "But I don't have a head here."

John, (11 years), tried —unsuccessfully—to explain to his parents that he was, "the space in which things happen."

These are true stories, and there are plenty more like them. Many children keep, even into their teens, a dwindling sense of their no-thingness and at-largeness as 1st person, of their citizenship of the Kingdom of Heaven (though not, of course, in these terms). And this is in spite of the fact that society in general, and the school in particular, exists to deny the 1st person, to cut everyone down to size, to turn them into loyal citizens of this world and mere 3rd persons.

No wonder, as the child grows up, his acquired view of himself-from-outside comes to overshadow, and in the end to obliterate, his native view of himself-from-inside. In fact, he grows *down*. At first he contained his world; now it contains him—what little there is of him. He takes everybody's word for what it's like where he is, except his own. The consequences are increasingly miserable. Shrunk from being the whole scene into being this contemptible part of it, he grows greedy, hating, fearful, closed in, and tired. Greedy, as he tries to regain at whatever cost a little of his own kingdom; hating, as he tries to revenge himself on a society that has cruelly made him feel so small; fearful, as he sees he is a mere thing up against all other things; closed in, because it is the nature of a thing to keep others out; tired, because so much energy goes in keeping up this thing's appearances instead of letting them go where they belong. And all these troubles arise from his basic trouble: his denial of this kingdom within, his identity-delusion, as he imagines (contrary to all the evidence) that he is to himself what he looks like to others—a lump of stuff. In short, he is beside himself, eccentric, self-alienated: so all goes wrong.

An outside view of himself is good and necessary. What is bad and unnecessary is the price he is made to pay for it—and to pay for damaged goods, at that. Not only *can* he see himself as the flesh, an object, without ceasing to see himself as spirit, the subject: *it is the only way he can do so without self-deception and self-reproach.* He learns far less painfully and far more thoroughly the essential lesson of his objective insignificance, his incurable imperfections, his weakness and incompetence and ignorance and brevity, if he remains alive also to what is nearer than all this—the Light, the indwelling Christ who suffers from no such limitations. Only from the strong fortress of the kingdom can he afford to admit to his peripheral, all-too-human vulnerability. Only by being truly great can he be truly humble. Not even a saint—let alone the average schoolboy—could wholeheartedly own to his short-comings if he were wholly identified with them.

What's needed are 'Schools for the Kingdom' —first, a prototype school, admittedly experimental, to be followed by many others, in which the child is *permitted* to remain a citizen of the kingdom. Permitted, not taught—as if such a subject could be on the curriculum! Of course, some children will want to forget their citizenship as soon as possible and grow up to be 'just like other people' , and of course they should be allowed to do that (or rather, to suppose they are doing it). But the avowed purpose of our school is to encourage children to preserve unbroken the thread of 1st-personhood right through from infancy to adulthood. The exceptional ones, who are already doing so in the existing system, show how normal the preservation of this life-line could be, given the school's support.

The teaching staff of our school will, for the most part, need to be people who are dedicated to that kingdom in which the child is naturally at home. Their task will be to help him balance, against the information he needs to gain, the wisdom that is his by birthright. In other words, to authorise his 2-way looking—simultaneously out at things and in at no-thing, the Light.

Not only is the child's needful and growing discovery of himself-as-a-thing (as 'flesh') eased and rectified by his continuing to see himself-as-no-thing (as 'spirit'), but his view of all other things, of the objective universe he studies at school, is rectified also. Thus the habitable and miraculous world of the kingdom of Heaven isn't denied in favour of the uninhabitable and common-sense world of social make-believe, but *both* are valued and explored, and the latter kept firmly in its place. The child treats his inner Light with infinite respect as the key to the cosmic puzzle, as his only reliable and accessible sample of how things really are. Acknowledging that he is *in appearance* particles, atoms, molecules, cells, a biological organism, a heavenly body, he sees himself to be *in reality* the crystal-clear Substratum of all these forms. And so his studies, whether in physics, chemistry, biology, sociology, geography or astronomy (disciplines at present so little related to himself and each other) are all of them partial answers to his question: 'What am I?' And he is himself, as the Light, the final answer to his question: 'What are they?' They are the manifold regional manifestations of that Source which he finds within himself, and which holds them together in unity. So he can truly say: "School is about me!"

Our "School for the Kingdom' can reasonably be expected to achieve, in some measure, the following results:

(1) Well-based mutual reverence —in particular, reverence for pupils by teachers, and readiness to learn from them as natives of the kingdom.

(2) Recognition by all that in the kingdom it is simplicity that counts, not cleverness.

(3) Liberation of the individual's unique gifts as he becomes more aware of their Source within.

(4) Reduction of the need to compensate for loss of the kingdom by greedy, aggressive, fearful behaviour, and by drug taking.

(5) Growing enjoyment of the One from whom flows infinite variety and the generosity to tolerate all its expressions.

REFERENCES

Prologue Mt 18.3 Gen 28.16,17
Game
1 Lk 10.21 Mk 10.14,15 Jn 16.13 Jn 14.16,17 Jn 8.32
2 Mt 18.3 Th 2 Lk 17,20,21
3a Lk 11.36 Th 23
3b Jn 12.24 Mt 10.39
4 Lk 11.34 Mt 7.5 Mk 9.47
5 Lk 8.16 Mt 10.26 Th 82 Th 77 Th 38
6 Mt 8.20 Jn 15.13 Mt 22.39
7 Mt 13.45,46
8 Mt 6.23 Mt 23.26,27 Th 60 Th 52
9 Th 91 Th 60 Mt 12.24
10 Th 60 Mt 11.29,30
11 Th 94 Mt 19.21ff
12 Mt 18.20 1Cor 3.16 Col 1.17,18
13 Jn 18.36 Jn 3.3ff Acts of John Rom 8.9 1Cor 12,13
14 Jn 8.12 Mt 5.14,15 Th 25
15 Th 106 Th 76 Mt 6.21
16 Th 29
17 Th 43 Lk 14.33 Mt 5.3 Jn 14.2
18 Th 38 2Cor 3.17ff
19a Mt 19.7 Jn 14.11 Th 15 Mt 5.8 Jn 16.25
19b 1Kings 19.11ff Ps 46.10
20 Mt 16.23 Jn 14.30 Mt 6.33

21 Th 51 Jas 1.17
22 Mt 18.8
23 Jn 5.30 Jn 14.10 Mt 10.19,20 Mt 6.33
24 Lk 15.11ff
25 Gen 1.1 Is 44.6 Ex 3.14 Th 1/ Gospel of Hebrews
26 Th 108 Th 18 Irenaus: Epideixis 43
27 Jn 5.43 Jn 8.58 Mt 28.20 Mt 25.35ff Rev 22.4
28 Ox Pap Th 6 Mt 10.29
29a Jn 10.9 Mt 7.7
29b Th 111 Lk 17.6 Th 103 Mt 17.20 Mt 19.26 Jn 14.14
30 Mt 13.15 Mt 8.3 Mt 10.7,8
31 Jn 6.63 Th 110 Mt 12.28 Jn 17.23
32 Jn 14.17 Jn 14.27 Jn 3.34
33 Jn 8.42 Jn 7.29 Th 51 Jn 4.14 Th 12
34 Jn 15.5 Th 77
35 Lk 11.34 Mt 26.26 Jn 6.51ff Th 105
36 Jn 18.37 Mt 10.38 Rom 6.6 Gal 2.20 1Cor 15.22

CPSIA information can be obtained
at www.ICGtesting.com
Printed in the USA
BVHW04s0734130318
510160BV00001B/71/P